LATENT IMAGE

LATENT IMAGE

Jack Eadon

VANTAGE PRESS
New York

This is a work of fiction. Any similarity between the characters appearing herein and any real persons, living or dead, is purely coincidental.

FIRST EDITION

All rights reserved, including the right of reproduction in whole or in part in any form.

Copyright © 2002 by Jack Eadon

Published by Vantage Press, Inc.
516 West 34th Street, New York, New York 10001

Manufactured in the United States of America
ISBN: 0-533-14080-3

Library of Congress Catalog Card No.: 01-126945

0 9 8 7 6 5 4 3 2 1

Acknowledgments

Thanks to Esther, my guiding light and editor, who inspires me with her desire for perfection but her tolerance for imperfection. Thanks also to my old friend Rita Markovics for her precision proofing and to the folks at Vantage for their continued support.

I dedicate this book to F. Scott Fitzgerald, who has always honored me with his vision and literacy. I humbly offer these pages to his spirit.

Finally, I thank Dancing Feather for her support, background information, and healing.

—Jack Eadon

LATENT IMAGE

Prologue

The Hike, Grand Canyon, Arizona, 1984

Suzanne drew back the natural cotton curtains and opened the windows centered on each wall of the adobe hut, letting in a soft breeze with the morning light. She called to her twin sister, Jessica, who tossed in bed, still half-asleep. Suzanne walked over and tapped her on her shoulder. "Come on, Jesse; don't waste your visit. You promised you'd go with me on a hike," she said. "Come on, please? It could be a life-altering experience for both of us. I swear, today we will see eagles soar. That's something you don't get to see in LA."

Suzanne returned to the simple wooden kitchen table and opened her backpack. In it she put a feather, a bundle of herbs, a small gourd bowl, a rolled-up woven mat, a little leather pouch, and a book of matches. She buckled the backpack closed with two leather straps.

"Eagles, schmeagles," Jessica mumbled into her pillow. "I don't buy all that spiritual crap."

"But, Jesse, I already packed for both of us. It's a little chilly out there, but the air is so clean. The canyon'll be like heaven."

"Ugh," Jessica groaned and started to rise, stopping to shine her nails on the sheet. "You're sure it won't wreck my hands? I've got this assignment coming up."

"You and your hand modeling. Come on, toots," Suzanne said.

"Okay, Okay."

"You'll see. We can hike to a special place Daniel showed me; it's like magic," Suzanne said. "Be a nice break from that LA pressure."

"Daniel Whitehorse, the medicine man? More of his Native American stuff, I bet."

"You ought to try getting into it, Jesse. He showed me a wonderful healing ceremony I'll share with you. As long as you promise not to tell." Suzanne poured some water into three plastic sports water bottles and attached them to her belt, a thick strip of Velcro on leather.

Jessica laughed cynically. "Like, who am I gonna tell?"

"Well, the details are sacred."

"Healing? I don't need any healing." Jessica got up and dressed, raking her fingers through her long, frizzy hair. "What'll we eat along the way? Trail mix, I suppose."

"Sure, it's good for you. You'll need the energy."

The two sisters left the room, bickering as usual, not realizing that after today their lives would never be the same.

1

Two years later, the Weston Restaurant, Costa Mesa, California, 1986

Marcus Ramsay weaved through the sparkling restaurant, barely avoiding the busy waiters. He rubbed his sore forearm as he pushed the leaves of tropical plants and scanned the tables—no Kathy.

Shit. Where the hell is she? Man, and I'm only a few minutes late.

Then he saw her sitting at a cloth-covered table for two, wearing her favorite gray suit and repeatedly glancing at her sterling silver watch. She was petite and stone-faced, and her dark eyes were flitting this way and that, framed by a sophisticated short hairstyle.

He walked up and leaned over the table. As he tried to give her a peck, she turned her cheek away.

He stood. "Hey, sorry I'm a little late." He swiped at his crumpled blue golf shirt.

"As usual," she said and looked at her watch.

"Well, jeez—just five minutes. I had to clean up. I was filthy from all the drywall dust." Ramsay had spent all day hanging drywall at his new photography studio.

"Your hair's getting too long," she said.

"Yeah, getting longer than yours." He half-laughed as he cleaned his dust-covered glasses, then futilely smoothed back his scraggly hair. He sat and looked out the floor-to-ceiling glass at the twinkling nighttime view of south Orange County from fifteen stories up. "Nice place."

"I guess." She sipped on her wine, little finger in the air. "How did you rip your shirt?"

"A nail."

She studied him. "God, and it's so faded. You must wear it every day."

"So?" He shrugged. "It's faded because I wash it a lot."

"Well, I remember when it was a classy *Izod* from Daddy. You've really wrecked it. Want some merlot?" she asked.

"Sure." He fumbled with the little *Izod* logo on his chest. He recalled those memories, too: the lake, the Sundays, her mom's iced tea and cookies.

Kathy Ramsay motioned to the waiter and pointed to Marcus's wineglass. The waiter took the bottle of Clos du Bois merlot, poured Marcus half a glass, refreshed hers, and set the bottle down.

Marcus swirled it. He raised his glass and smiled. "To you, Munchkin. Long time no see."

"Don't call me that," she said tersely.

"You used to like it."

"I never liked it," Kathy snapped.

"I always thought you did," he said. Ramsay felt stung by her hard-edged response.

"I guess you weren't paying attention," she said and held up her menu.

"Man, do I sense a little coolness?" He leaned forward, figuring it was time to make his plea before things got any rougher. "This separation stuff sucks, Kathy," he said. "I'm tired of the apartment bit; it's like I'm single. I think we should get back together." He grabbed his cloth napkin, unfolded it, and tossed it across his lap. "This has been long enough."

They ordered their food.

"Seven weeks? The photo studio having trouble already?" she asked. "What did you do to your arm anyway? It looks awful."

He lightly pressed the large contusion on his right forearm. "A two-by-four fell onto it when I wasn't looking. It'll be okay—a little sore." Ramsay had never supervised a construction finish-out before, having been a corporate marketeer. He felt a bit out of his element in a commercial photo studio.

He saw a small smile appear on her face. "What is it?" he asked.

"You haven't even signed the lease yet," she snickered. "Is getting banged up part of your new photo life?"

"I hope not. I'm rushing the finish-out since the lease starts Monday. Good time to get back together, don't you think?"

"I don't know. We ought to give it a little time. It sounds to me like you're feeling a little dependent, maybe after getting fired and starting the photo thing. That's what Daddy predicted would happen. He thinks you just ought to shake it off and move on."

Ramsay thought back to his dismissal from the Puritan Corporation a few months earlier. "I don't care what your daddy thinks," he said. "I just want us to work. How the hell would he know how I feel, anyway? One minute, I was on the way up at Puritan; the next . . . discarded. Has he ever been through that?"

"Daddy? Unlikely. Still, he thinks you carry your deal on your sleeve. I do, too. You probably overestimated your potential there all along."

"How would you know? Hickman'll have to live with firing me forever." Earl Hickman, the president and his boss, had fired Marcus when his upper-management supporters from Chicago headquarters were away at their annual sales meeting in Phoenix. Marcus had always thought the timing for his dismissal was a little suspect.

"You should've bitched right away instead of acting so blasé. You were so self-righteous. 'I want to be the honorable man,' you kept saying. I've never heard of such nonsense. You should've sued them."

"Bull. They can get away with anything they want to in the Abyss. Texas is a *right-to-work* state, anyway—that makes it even easier for them to do stuff like that." He hung his head.

"You probably just need my financial support for your photo thing, right?" She shook her head. "Nice future."

The waiter served a Caesar Salad-for-two they had ordered—one of their old traditions.

"Man. I hate when you call it that," he said. "The photo thing. It's a studio, Kathy. It's an advertising photography studio—my new life. We agreed to give this a shot."

She shook her head. "I guess. But it was only if your so-called sponsors at Puritan didn't save you first, which they were supposed to, according to you. Remember?"

Ramsay looked away, feeling a flush. *She's right,* he thought. All his dreams at Puritan had ended up illusions in the end. All that was good about the company—the security, the tradition, the loyalty—had evaporated in an instant. And there were never any white knights that appeared to rescue him from being cast away.

"Maybe you'll be better at the photo thing. You've

worked hard enough mastering that light painting technique; that's for sure. Maybe the clients out here in la-la land'll even like it."

"Expect so." Ramsay puffed up, confident, thinking that California was, indeed, the perfect spot for his new style of lighting.

"That's if they buy into doing arty photography for medical gadgets."

He exhaled. "God, Kathy, you really make it sound iffy," he said. After he was fired, Ramsay had practiced his longtime photographic avocation in his garage studio for hours. He had perfected a technique for lighting that could be applied to the photography of any product, including the medical gizmos that represented most of the advertising photography business in Orange County. His midnight sessions had paid off, he reckoned.

He had noticed in the photo press that other photographers across the country were experimenting with the same sort of light painting idea. One in particular, the technique's creator, Aaron Jones, based in San Francisco, then Santa Fe, had made it his specialty. Few except Aaron had managed to make the technique popular with their clients.

The waiter came back and cleared his throat. "Excuse me. Pepper on your half, ma'am?" he asked.

She shook her head.

"You, sir?"

"A little."

The waiter dispensed the pepper and disappeared.

"The studio's twenty-five hundred a month, too. Like another mortgage," she said. She sighed as she took a forkful of the salad.

"It won't be a problem when the business gets going,"

he said. "My day rate's fifteen hundred."

"Gets going. Whenever that is." She rolled her eyes. "I thought you said Orange County was crawling with old pro photographers, too. Do you really think they're going to give you their business without a fight? Or is that more of your wishful thinking? Anyway, I still think this photo thing is just a diversion to keep you from getting on with your real life."

"Kathy, I never deserved to get axed. It never should've happened—it wasn't fair. I'll never trust the Abyss again."

"Denial." Kathy mumbled as she looked away. "If there wasn't some reason for Earl letting you go, he wouldn't have. Your time there was probably over. And there's no such thing as fair."

"Thanks." Ramsay slurped some water. "More bullshit from Daddy, I bet."

She scrunched her nose. "Just learn from it and let it go."

Marcus stabbed at a crouton with his fork. Then he put it, dripping with Caesar Dressing, into his mouth. "Well, I'm sorry, but I can't picture being without you anymore," he said as he chewed. "We should get over this bull and make a new start."

Kathy Ramsay blandly stabbed at another crouton. "Marcus, with you doing the photo thing, and me at . . ." She tapped her finger. "Don't you see?"

"Are you being so cut-and-dried because you're now a fancy director of marketing?" he asked. "Is that more fluff from the Abyss?"

"Stop calling corporate life the Abyss," she said. "Just because you blew it there."

"Bitch," Ramsay whispered as Kathy's words sank in. a drip of dressing fell to his lap. He wiped it away with his napkin. "I guess it's your upbringing," he mumbled sarcastically. While his background was struggling lower-middle-class, Kathy's was one of privilege, spawned by her dad's upper-management position at a Fortune 500 company.

"What's wrong with my upbringing?" she sneered.

She doesn't get it, he thought. Just then he recognized the fissure that must've been there all along. "It's been the institutionalization of Kathy Ramsay since the day she was born. You've always seen the world in black-and-white, a fixed set of rules from the Abyss, and now that includes how you see me."

"So?" She jabbed at the last crouton at the same time he did. They dueled over it for five seconds, their forks tiny swords, until, apparently unmoved, she casually put her fork down. "Take it. I don't want it anymore."

Minutes later, outside the Weston, Marcus Ramsay, breathing hard, hurriedly tipped the valet and got into his car. He couldn't believe how after only seven weeks Kathy seemed eager to categorize him as hopeless, forgetting the team that they had been: acting like they had never gone to the "promontory point" on Chicago's South Side for picnics and had never taken long walks along Lake Michigan; as if they had never kissed and danced in Lincoln Park, surrounded by squirrels, leaves, and, depending on the season, an occasional Canada goose.

Later that night at his apartment in Tustin, Ramsay heated some herbal tea. As the tea freed his blocked sinuses, he thought back to Texas, to the night Earl Hickman had snickered as he dumped him, even after Ramsay had made him and his Texas cronies look so good to the Puritan brass back in Chicago.

"Y'all's job is over," Earl had said that night. "Every damn thing around here is new. We don't want any more changes."

At that moment Ramsay had felt torn apart. He had struggled so hard to make a difference for the little division of Puritan. He figured his achievements had been so stunning that they would surely propel him upward through the corporation. But after he was fired, he was apparently ignored by his alleged sponsors back at Puritan in Chicago. They were too busy in Phoenix, playing golf and celebrating their awful scores with off-color jokes and stiff margaritas.

Now he was trying a new career as an advertising photographer in a new location—Orange County, California. He knew it would take more than guts, so before he moved from Texas he worked hard in his makeshift garage-studio, developing innovative ideas about photographic lighting.

After a year of nightly practice, his experimentation germinated into practical methods that could bolster his new endeavor. Despite his technical success, though, he knew he would be fulfilled only if he could rehab his married life, too.

Ramsay fell into bed thinking of Kathy, imagining her stopping by his new studio after work and catching a bite with him at the Barn, a restaurant across the street: he, the successful advertising photographer; she, the hard-charging executive at Pepe's Café headquarters.

He turned out the light but lay awake for several

hours. He imagined the same dinner over and over. The more he imagined it, the more he could picture Kathy arriving late or not at all.

2

Marcus Ramsay Photographic, Tustin, California

The next day Ramsay drove his Jeep through a maze of industrial commercial suites—four to a building—in Tustin's Cole Business Park. He turned a corner and pulled to a stop in front of Suite B, the 15031 building, MARCUS RAMSAY PHOTOGRAPHIC on the door in white, bold letters.

He liked how his name sounded. Orange County advertising photographers, much like models, would usually change their names to give them a "show-biz" sound, but Ramsay knew that wouldn't be necessary in his case—*Marcus Ramsay* was perfect.

As he unlocked the front door, he heard the prerecorded reveille sound at the Tustin Marine Helicopter Base, situated next to the business park. Once inside, he passed through his spare reception area, turned left, and walked through the client lounge. Rows of his sixteen-by-twenty-inch photographs hung on the wall, each exhibiting his light painting technique. *Not bad,* he thought.

He walked into his office. Piles of moving boxes still surrounded his desk. He left his battered briefcase next to the desk and walked back through the client lounge to the door labeled: STUDIO. He opened it.

Once he was inside, the closing door echoed through the 2,000 square feet of empty studio, forty feet wide by fifty feet long, dimly lit by a few "ambient" lights hung high on each wall. The floor was painted a shiny, pale blue epoxy. The ceiling was flat black. The walls were new gallery white.

A "monopod" camera stand, a black fourteen-foot-tall, six-inch-diameter shaft, towered over a handful of suitcase-sized power packs in the center of the studio. The stand cradled Ramsay's four-by-five camera, a professional bellows-type affair. *The best stuff in the best place*, he thought.

Stan Devlin had endorsed Ramsay's choice of equipment, and Stan was the area's leading advertising photographer, one of the "old guard." Having Stan's endorsement had given Ramsay some level of confidence that his new venture wouldn't be just an escape from his failed past, but a truly successful future. Ramsay took a few steps forward and stood like a genie, arms folded, and beheld his equipment. "Yes, sir. Looks pretty damn good," he mumbled.

"Sure does," a crackly voice behind him said.

Ramsay turned around. The studio door was ajar. The silhouette of a robust figure stood in it.

"Hi," Ramsay said to the figure. "Don't believe we've met."

Out of the shadows stepped an older fellow with white hair, a friendly-looking pear-shaped face, and a stocky frame. He waddled forward. "Aloha," he said. "I'm Donald McKenzie. Your neighbor."

"Sycamore Studios?" Ramsay said. "I hear you've been there awhile."

"Ten years, since the fire at the old place." He kept waddling forward.

"Fire?"

"We used to be over there on Sycamore Street." He pointed. "Place burnt down."

"What do you guys do over there?" Ramsay asked.

They shook hands.

"Prepress."

"What's that?"

"Halftone film, plates—all that. In my younger years, I used to shoot ads like you."

"Oh?"

He laughed. "Long time ago, back in Honolulu. Grew up there. Your place looks great, by the way. Nice equipment," McKenzie said.

"Thanks. Hopefully I can get some business to pay for it. Should I call you Don?"

"Everybody calls me Donald. It's pretty competitive around here, you know," McKenzie said. "Lots of guys with studios."

"I'm doing a new kind of lighting. Maybe the clients'll like it," Ramsay said.

"Oh, yeah?"

"It's called light painting."

"What's so special about it?"

"Looks like a painting. I shoot in a near-dark studio, open the camera lens, and apply light to the subject with a little fiber-optic wand."

"I get it. Like those shots out there?" Donald pointed back to the client lounge.

Ramsay nodded.

"Gosh, I wasn't sure they were photographs," McKenzie said. "Real nice."

"Thanks. I hope the clients agree."

Later that day, as Ramsay practiced his light painting technique alone in the dark, the studio door was nudged open.

"Oops! Please close the door," he said.

"Sorry." A willowy woman quickly closed the door. "Hi, I'm Amy Baker. Backman Medical? Right down Red Hill."

"Nice to meet you. What can I do for you?" Ramsay asked. On the surface, Amy was just another female corporate type like Kathy.

"Heard you were the new shooter in town. I thought I'd stop by. Those your images out there?"

"Yeah," he said. He turned on the ambient studio lights.

"Really nice." She walked up to Ramsay. Her black, short-cropped hair crowned a crisp, blue business suit.

"Glad you like 'em."

"I'm the art director over there."

Potential business? Ramsay thought, smoothing his hair.

"Work's great." The studio lights shot across her hard, angular face. "Been using the local guys for years, but their work isn't as edgy as yours."

"Edgy? Thanks, I guess. What do you need photographed?"

"Small medical equipment for ads, brochures, and trade show materials."

"Cool. High-tech product shooting is my specialty."

"Care to shoot for us sometime?" she asked. "Your style's sort of artsy. It could help give us a spin against the competition. For the most part, an oxygenator looks like an oxygenator, right?"

"I'll be set up soon," Ramsay said.

"Well, when?" Her monotone voice sounded all business.

"Couple of weeks, max. Have to tweak the lighting a bit, but you can count on me."

"When you're ready, call." She presented her card and looked around. "Nice work environment here."

"I didn't expect any walk-in business, Amy. This is great."

"Oh, one more thing." She raised her index finger, exhibiting a perfect red nail.

"What is it?" he asked. Ramsay thought, *Here's the catch.*

"Don't believe anything you hear about me from the other guys," she said.

He laughed uneasily. "Like what?"

"They complain about me, but I'm not that hard to work with."

"So, you're the prototypical art director from hell?" He laughed uneasily.

She didn't. "Sort of. Bye." As she turned and walked out, the clicking of her heels echoed through the studio.

That night Ramsay ate a couple of soft tacos at a Pepe's Café on Newport Avenue, several blocks from his apartment. As he munched, he thought about Amy Baker. She seemed nice but cut-and-dried, too. Was she the type he'd be working with as he did his photo thing? One of those folks from the Abyss he involuntarily left behind?

Later, as Ramsay lay on the couch in his apartment, he contemplated that since he wasn't due to sign his lease until Monday, he could still bail out of the whole photography venture. But then the Cole Company would hit him with a bill for thousands of dollars to undo the remodeling he had already completed. That would irk Kathy for years!

By the time Ramsay was dressing for bed, he had eliminated the "bail-out" option from consideration, but he still felt queasy—maybe it was the tacos.

3

Stan Devlin Photography, Newport Beach, California

The next morning Stan Devlin sat at the head of the conference room table in his studio in Newport Beach.

"So, Stan, what's all the urgency about getting together?" Ken Potter asked as he stroked his white beard. "Does this take the place of the SIP board meeting?"

"No, I thought we should talk about paying close attention to this new dude down the street. We really don't need any more competition, least of all a hotshot like Marcus Ramsay." Stan was about forty-five, a squat man with closely set slits for eyes that sat high on his flat, rectangular face. His stubby arms flapped as he talked. In another era he could have been a great egocentric general, so sure was he as he addressed his buddies.

"Listen. I've been around here for twenty years," Stan said. His eyelid slits squinted further. "We've had our troubles, but there's never been trouble like this."

"What's the big deal?" Potter asked.

"I don't want to lay the sympathy bit on your guys," Stan said, "but if Amy Baker goes for this guy, I could lose Backman."

Potter raised his eyebrows. It had been Stan's account for years. "It does look a little neat out in your studio, Stan. A little slow recently?"

Stan tapped his fingers loudly. "You know Backman's

been thirty percent of my damned billings," he said. "You figure it out. And I happen to know she's already saving their next big job for Ramsay."

All at once the rest of the group lowered their heads. It was rare that Stan Devlin spoke in such an urgent, fearful tone.

"What's so special about him?" Art Zipper grunted like a monkey and fidgeted in his chair.

"That light painting," Stan said. "I happen to know that Amy went over to visit him yesterday. When was the last time she went over to your studios?"

"Man-oh-man," Steve Gerard grumbled. Steve was the youngest of the bunch. Formerly the newcomer, he had been accepted by the rest after he had raised his prices and stopped discounting to new clients.

"You know, I think it's time we did something about guys like him," Devlin said. "There's more and more of 'em every day."

"That's right, Stan," Art Zipper grunted and scratched his upper torso. "Conroy said he got one of Ramsay's bullshit promo pieces in the mail."

Steve Gerard jumped in. "Holmes'll give him a chance. He tries everybody new in town. That's fifty thousand dollars in billings gone every year if I lose him. That would cover my rent."

Among them—Stan Devlin, Ken Potter, Art Zipper, Steve Gerard, and James Honeybear—they had logged a hundred years of shooting advertising photographs in burgeoning Orange County. Some of them, like Honeybear, born James Beresford, had picked stage names that would be easier for clients to remember. Honeybear had picked his name to add warmth to his aloof personality, made particularly intimidating by his linebacker frame and unyielding demeanor.

Based on what they were all shooting, the newer shooters in Orange County, especially this Marcus Ramsay, were bound to steal away the dreams they had for their businesses. Potter shifted his eyes back and forth. Gerard mirrored him.

"Well, something has to be done to slow down Ramsay," Devlin said

Art Zipper squeaked excitedly.

"But, Stan, you aren't advocating violence, are you?" Potter stroked his beard.

"Naw. Relax, Ken. We just need to make it a little tough on him," Devlin said, "though I admit I'd love to make the asshole disappear."

"How, Stan?" Art Zipper mumbled dumbly. "Get a little heavy?" Zipper rubbed his severely scarred forearm. A demolition wound had sent him home from Vietnam with a Purple Heart.

"Naw, but remember, when we opened, there were no good clients, so we can start there. I can talk to Amy. And the rent—it was a killer. Remember the initial expenses of running a studio, too. Man!"

"Stan, you gonna control his rent?" Art Zipper asked. He got a little more animated. He rocked back and forth, rubbed his hands together, and scratched his nose. "And how we gonna add to the other expenses?"

"First off, his studio's in the right business park," Devlin said as he lowered his voice. He looked around as if someone else was listening. "He took my suggestion about where to set up." He smiled slyly.

"Cole?" Potter asked.

Stan nodded. "The one in Tustin."

Zipper chattered excitedly.

"He's got a five-year deal over there."

"That'll lock him in," Zipper said. "Those Cole folks'll kill him with their extra maintenance fees."

"What about his other expenses?" Gerard asked.

"We can make sure he gets hit with lots of surprises, but I'll have to think on that," Devlin said and shrugged. "We just want to keep things fair."

When Stan talked about what was fair for Orange County advertising photographers, he spoke with a certain self-righteousness the others liked. When they nodded, he knew his plan rang with credibility.

"We just got to get things back to where they used to be," Art Zipper said as he threw a vague salute. He had been Stan's major supporter ever since he had returned to the States with his Purple Heart. After he recovered, Art had used the money from the GI Bill to attend photo school at the Brooks Institute up in Santa Barbara. Then he returned to Orange County and opened his studio about the same time as Stan, just when the county's growth took off.

"All these new guys around here are pushing rates down," Gerard said.

"We've just got to educate them," Potter said. He was the oldest member of the group, having studioed up in LA before heading south to Orange County. At meetings like this one, he usually stayed quiet until the others had their say. Then he formulated a point of view on the spot that combined their opinions. Therefore, he always sounded particularly wise.

"What about SIP?" Gerard asked.

"Of course," Devlin said. "Gotta get him to join."

"Course," Potter grumbled and fiddled with his beard.

"What's the matter, James?" Stan asked.

"I don't know. This sounds like Nazi stuff, Stan. No offense. Ramsay and the rest are just starting. I remember when we did the same crap with Gerard when he started."

"And look," Devlin said. "Steve's one of us now, right?" He pointed to Gerard.

"But still, this sounds a little nasty," Potter said.

Devlin silently seethed at Potter's response. Then he slapped the table and shouted, "Ken, I'm surprised at you! You're normally responsible. Did you know Ramsay used to be on the client side?"

"Huh?" Potter looked up. His tough attitude toward clients was legendary.

Devlin nodded. "Yes, sir. He told me he used to work at the Puritan Corporation. He ran a division of theirs in Texas. He has an MBA, too—this guy's no dummy," Devlin said.

"Really?" Potter said. He flushed a little as he scratched his beard.

"It's easy to imagine that kind of shooter taking over Orange County photography," Steve Gerard said. "It's so different than when we started—we were just shooters. He's a shooter *and* a suit."

Stan leaned forward. "You guys know a recession is coming to Orange County, right? Could be a threat to our businesses." He faced Potter. "Including yours."

Ken fidgeted.

Stan continued, "Joan says some of them hotshot MBA bean counters even took over the Pacific Symphony Orchestra and fired some of the senior folks."

"The PSA?" Potter winced. "Shoot."

"Yeah, they fired cellos. Can you imagine, Ken? Cellos? Joan was third chair; now she's first, but at the same salary. Fifteen years there . . . and she'll be the next to go—fucking bean counters."

"Shit," Potter said. "I didn't know, Stan. Sorry."

"It could be a crisis for the Devlins; my business, Joan's job, the house."

"Thanks to guys like this Ramsay dude, huh?" Zipper grunted.

"And Ramsay's wife, too. She's a big shot over at Pepe's Café headquarters. Another MBA."

Zipper cringed. "I hate those bastards."

There was silence.

Devlin scanned the group's hanging heads. He had made a good case.

Then Ken Potter spoke as he pointed to the photographs on each of the walls. "Stan, are you sure you're not just bitching about Ramsay because he shoots high-tech stuff, like you? He'll probably steal a lot more of your business than ours."

"Fuck you, Ken," Devlin grumbled.

"Well, I'm just saying. Maybe it's just a power thing," Potter said. "You might not be the photo god around here anymore. Now you'll have some fancy light painting MBA competition." He snickered and looked around the room. "Must piss you off."

Devlin fumed at Potter's relaxed façade. He took a condescending demeanor and started to talk soothingly. "Ramsay supposedly does that new light painting stuff on high-tech products, right?" Then he slowly raised his voice and, as he did, flushed. "But he can use his technique to shoot *any* product, not just high-tech. Up in San Francisco, Aaron Jones even shoots cars! And they're eatin' it up. Doesn't that concern you?" He looked at Ken, then up and down the table. "Just imagine what Ramsay might pull next: food, medical—whatever!"

They grumbled.

Devlin's studio manager appeared at the door, holding a coffeepot. "You guys want more?" she asked.

"Not now, Rita." Devlin waved her away, then turned back to his friends. "Ramsay even learned by himself back in Texas," he said. "He could be a real natural."

"You mean he never went to photo school?" Potter asked. "Brooks? Rochester?"

"No, but he's good. I've seen his book," Devlin said. "He shoots like Aaron Jones."

"Is he a nice guy?" James Honeybear asked.

Devlin smirked. "Nice guy? You should have seen him looking around at my studio, asking a lot of questions. Like he expected me to tell him everything I know. So, I'm thinking we should plant someone close to him to keep an eye on him, report back to us. What do you think?"

"Whew!" Art Zipper said. He rubbed his hands together. "This sounds pretty heavy."

"Zipper! You like anything heavy," Steve Gerard said and laughed.

Zipper hissed at Gerard.

"Listen, Ramsay's bound to hurt us if we don't do something fast," Devlin said. "Losing Backman would only be the beginning for me. Maybe the end."

"Wait a minute. How would planting somebody in his studio help?" James Honeybear asked. "Sounds ridiculous."

"Keeping an eye on him, James. That's all. Report back to us. Seems like a smart thing to do right now. Listen, what we're talking about is staying in business, right? Maybe we can make things a little tough for him—it's only fair."

"Did Ramsay protest the war?" Art Zipper's eyes winced. "He's not one of them, is he?"

"Don't blow a gut, Art," Devlin said. "We gotta keep things logical here. If we can, we should get a studio manager or assistant in there. I got a few ideas."

"Well, I hate those hippie types," Zipper said. "All I'm saying is that they protested back home while the rest of us got shot up in that hell."

"Easy, Zipper, easy," Potter said.

"Well, is Ramsay like that, Stan? I hate those assholes."

James Honeybear cleared his throat. "I've been listening to you guys rant and rave over someone that only Stan's met. The guy might be a real nice guy."

"Yeah, but he even looks like an MBA. Right, Stan?" Art Zipper said. "How could a *suit* be a nice guy?"

Honeybear smirked at Zipper. "Still, I think it's sort of strange that we're talking like this. It's McCarthyism—nothing less. We can't do all of this just to satisfy power mongering by certain shooters with obvious ego crises." He turned to Devlin. "Right, Stan?"

Devlin had never liked James Honeybear's cool, sophisticated exterior, Hollywood name, and now, obvious attack. "Listen, James. Pepe's Café is your client, right? How long have you been shooting for them? Five years? Ten? You want to lose that business? How many thousands is that every year? What percent of your billings? Your showy name won't protect you against Ramsay."

"He has a point, James," Potter said.

Devlin watched Honeybear shake his large head. "Come on, Honeybear; when are you going to stand up with us instead of a damned MBA outsider like this Ramsay dude? You don't even know him."

"Well—," Honeybear said. "I guess—"

"Stan," Ken Potter jumped in again, "I can see your point about keeping an eye on Ramsay, maybe making it a little tough. I agree in principle. As long as there's no rough stuff."

"No one ever said rough," Devlin said.

"I still think this is a bit far-fetched," James Honeybear said. "I don't know."

"It's just reality, James," Devlin said. "We've stuck together on the pricing and it's worked."

"True. But discussing pricing at the SIP meetings has been the main help," Honeybear said.

"True. So, we need to get Ramsay to join SIP," Art Zipper said, finger raised. "He could hear about keeping rates up, all that." The Society of Illustrative Photographers had been started by Devlin years before to peg rates uniformly high in Orange County. The organization had a strong foothold, bordering on unionism.

"Good idea, Art," Potter said. "Keep him close."

"Maybe down the road," Devlin said, "we could even make him president. Stop him from stealing business from us, he'd be so busy running SIP."

Zipper "eeked." "Pretty cool. Make him president, slow him down—pretty sly, Stan." Zipper rubbed his hands together again.

"For now we're agreed to keep an eye on him, then,"

Stan Devlin said. "Sort of a test case—I'll manage it. I'll just need a few hundred bucks from each of you to start. Maybe a little more later."

"I still think this whole thing is a bit underhanded," James Honeybear said. "But I guess I'll go along for a few months."

Art Zipper saluted with a relaxed crooked hand, like an old infantryman. His tone was important, like his approval really mattered. "I'm in."

"Me, too," most of the others mumbled.

"That's more like it," Stan Devlin said, and smiled.

4

Marcus Ramsay Photographic

Minutes later the same morning, on the other side of the 405 freeway, Marcus Ramsay sat in his office and fiddled with his computer. He leaned over and pulled out a yellowed memo from his old briefcase. It was from Bill Brownburg, the president of Puritan's food division during most of Ramsay's years there, before the man died of an unexpected heart attack. It was written to the personnel vice president on the occasion of Ramsay being hired at Puritan. He had kept it in his briefcase for years and often read it. "Looks like we have a real communicator here," Brownburg had written. "Let's get him on board." Just as Ramsay finished reading the hand-written note, the front doorbell to his studio rang and, moments later, Donald McKenzie appeared at his office door.

"Say, Marcus, got a little present for you," he said.

"Oh?"

He walked forward, tossed an old sepia-toned photograph on Ramsay's desk, and stood there grinning, hands on hips.

"What's this?" Ramsay asked. He picked it up as he studied it.

"The original place."

"When it was on Sycamore?"

"Yeah. Before the fire." The old guy looked proud.

"Cool," Ramsay said.

"It'll be good luck for your start-up," McKenzie said.

"Hey, thanks. That's really special, but I can't accept—"

"No, I have another. This one's for you."

"And Sycamore's still going after twenty-five years?"

"See, there's hope," McKenzie said. "Fifteen years after the fire."

"Honestly, it's still not too late to pull out of this whole deal," Ramsay said.

"What about your lighting technique? Pretty special, right?"

"Just having my doubts, I guess. Couldn't sleep all weekend. Felt stage fright in my gut."

"But you said you spent a lot of time perfecting that lighting back in Texas, right?"

"I was sort of obsessed, I guess," Ramsay said.

The doorbell interrupted them.

"Back here!" Ramsay shouted. "What is this? Grand Central Station?" he said.

In a second, a gangly young man in an orange T-shirt and baggy shorts appeared at the office door. "You Marcus Ramsay?"

"That's me. What can I do for you?"

"Just sign right here." He walked in and handed Ramsay a pink receipt and a thick packet.

Ramsay signed the voucher, handed it back, and inspected the thick nine-by-twelve cardboard envelope. "Wonder what this is? Just a second, Donald."

"No problem." The old guy stood in place. "Looks important."

Ramsay tore open the envelope. "Official-looking," he

said. As he skimmed the pages, his chest tightened. He sucked in a breath. "Oh, my God."

"What is it?" Donald asked. "Are you okay?"

"Papers. She served me." Without a word Ramsay swiveled and reached for the phone. "Wait a second, Donald," Ramsay said. "Is she there?" he asked.

"This is Susan," the voice said. "Can I help you?"

"Listen, Susan, I just got something delivered—"

"The papers?"

Ramsay paused. "She's telling everyone? I don't believe it."

"Kathy said if you called, I should say they'd be self-explanatory."

Ramsay flushed. "I can't believe it."

"Should I have her call you?" Susan asked.

"Not necessary, I guess. Bye."

Ramsay put down the phone.

"What is it?" Donald asked. "You look pale."

"My wife served me," Ramsay said. "And I just had dinner with her. I thought we'd be getting back together—what a fool."

"Hey, I'm sorry," McKenzie said.

"I bet she was already planning this."

"That's awful," Donald said, shaking his head.

"What am I going to do? I can't sign the damn lease. If I don't have a marriage, I don't have a business. We agreed to give this a go. How am I gonna live?"

"You need some time. Maybe I better leave, huh?" Donald said. He turned and started walking away.

"No, Donald. Wait." Ramsay fiddled with Donald's old sepia-toned picture. "I could use your advice." Ramsay's breathing was a bit labored. "You have any ideas about how I can get out of this rut?"

"The lease?" Donald turned back. "You haven't signed it, right?" He shrugged and paused. "So, you're not stuck."

"But all the build-out I've done," Ramsay said. "I couldn't possibly afford to undo all this."

"Right. Well, you could go for it, I s'pose," Donald said, pointing around the office.

"But I'm just starting. No financial backup. She was gonna be the safety net for our new life."

"You got that lighting technique, right?" McKenzie asked. "Pretty darn good."

"I guess." Ramsay sighed deeply. He slammed the desk in frustration. "Man, how could she do this? I should have seen this coming."

"I got divorced once," Donald said. "We both changed."

"What'd you do?" Ramsay asked.

"At first I was angry and shocked," Donald said. "Doubted myself for a couple of years. Then I got it back together and met Helen."

"A couple of years? Wow."

"Helen's great, though. Definitely worth the wait."

"Couple of years?"

"Don't worry; you'll recoup. You gotta have faith. Accept your losses and move on." He wagged his finger. "Helen? She's the best."

Ramsay hesitated, glancing at the two piles before him: the lease documents and the divorce papers. "It's so final," he said. "After ten years." Ramsay tapped his pen in thought. "Man, and I'd be stuck here for five years."

"What's five years?" McKenzie asked.

"The lease is a hundred-fifty-thousand-dollar commitment. If I blow it, I'll be in hock forever."

"Hmm. Still think you oughta do it, maybe," Donald said. "That lighting style will do it, I bet. Five years'll come and go before you know it. Might even find a new lady by then."

Ramsay picked up his pen and wiggled it, thinking. "Last week I did figure I was in the right place at the right time. But a hundred-fifty grand?" He glanced at Donald's old picture. Then he looked up at him. "So, you even made it despite the fire?"

"Yep." He seemed to recall it for a second. "But I got over it all. You can, too." Donald smiled. "Just got to commit, then go for it."

Ramsay looked back at his stacks of papers, thought of Kathy, and sniffed a tear. He took the cap off his pen. Without stopping, he scribbled his signature in what seemed like a million spaces on the divorce papers and the lease.

"There." He recapped his pen and tossed it down. "I can't believe I did that."

"Congratulations, you're in business." Donald smiled.

"Not quite," Marcus said. He dug a business card out of his wallet, picked up the phone, and dialed.

"Amy Baker," a voice answered.

"Amy?"

"Yes? Who is it?"

"Marcus Ramsay here. I called to take you up on that assignment."

"But I thought you weren't ready," she said.

"Something came up," he said. "I'll only need a week to get ready."

Early Monday evening the chilly marine layer drifted into Laguna Beach from the Pacific Ocean. Stan Devlin loved the stroll from downtown Laguna Beach, where two locals had just started a pickup game at the basketball court on the main beach, near the business district on Pacific Coast Highway—locals called it PCH. Devlin had lived in Laguna Beach, Orange County's artists' haven, since he graduated from photo school. Strolling along the beach every evening with his dog, Rusty, had become as regular as brushing his teeth. He looked forward to that time to reflect on his day.

He hurled a flat stone at the steely ocean but was unable to skim it across the calm water like he used to. It made contact twice before *kerplunking* into a faint twilight wave.

"Rusty!" It was time to head home for dinner. Devlin's dog lumbered up, kicking damp sand. Joan was at home, making her beef stew, perfect for clammy evenings when the fog enveloped the town and left misty rings of light encircling the old street lamps.

Stan Devlin reviewed his life-collective—born in an era characterized by high photography fees, limited competition, and a bounty of clients which was now being threatened. For his dreams to come true, he would have to intervene.

For ten years he had appreciated the silent kudos he received when he wandered into Perry's Camera or Datachrome—the best of the local photo labs—as the youthful body politic of Orange County commercial photography recognized him and paid him awestruck homage with indistinct whispers. Nowadays, a few more of them failed to recognize him each time he visited one of the local establishments. He felt his fame slipping away.

Was it because he was now in his forties and life was flying by? Was he no longer in touch with the younger shooters because he was the father of a seven-year-old daughter or the husband of a concert cellist? Had the world just changed—different catch phrases, daily priorities, and favorite radio stations? Signs were all around that things weren't the same as they used to be.

Stan Devlin knew he didn't like that faltering feeling. He congratulated himself for deciding to take steps to control his fate rather than let happenstance dump him into an unsatisfactory future. He reached down for one last stone and flung it with a little more finesse.

Kerplunk! "Oh, well." He felt wise enough to successfully refurbish a life design not yet realized. "Rusty, let's go home—see Mommy and Tracy," he said.

Devlin leashed his dog, ignoring tugs of protest from the wandering canine head, and strolled down PCH past a steady line of rush-hour cars streaming through Laguna. He and Rusty crossed at Bluebird Canyon Road and walked up the hill to his weathered, white-frame, two-bedroom house.

He felt good about rallying his buddies against Marcus Ramsay, the most cancerous of the intruding shooters. Ramsay looked capable of leading Orange County photographers in ways of thinking about photography that were new and confusing. *Light painting technique? Business acumen? Fucking MBA!*

Devlin thought about his bold commitment to his buddies. He would hire someone to infiltrate Ramsay's studio to undermine his efforts. Now that Devlin had discovered that Amy would be hiring Ramsay for an upcoming assignment, the undermining notion was no longer a vague idea. It was an on-target one.

But whom could he recruit? At what cost? He knew he'd need to find someone intelligent and discreet, crafty and witty, capable of thinking on his feet. Devlin already had someone in mind.

As he approached the house, he smelled the ripe odors of the beef stew recipe Joan had gotten from his mother years before. Rusty barked, recognizing familiar smells on the sidewalk. Devlin felt a pang of excitement as he pondered his colorful future, saturated with a vivid palette of unknown hues.

By actively subjugating Ramsay he would be able to track the man's progress and limit it in ways he had yet to contrive—Devlin, the puppeteer. If he planned well, he would retain his unofficial position as the leader of all Orange County photographers. No one, especially this Marcus Ramsay character with his fancy lighting and corporate background, would take that way from him. Stan Devlin would make sure of that.

Meanwhile, in his tiny, dark living room, Marcus Ramsay sulked in the lone easy chair. He listened to the mindless jabber on the TV. The ceiling fan sputtered, sounding out-of-phase, like there were two motors running at slightly out-of-sync speeds. Ramsay was still shaky from having received the divorce papers from Kathy. As a new emptiness descended upon him, he wondered if he had ever been truly worthy of her or the Abyss. His losses in both arenas seemed inexplicably linked—first his corporate firing, then the divorce. Now they seemed like adjacent dominoes falling, one after the other. Would his uncertain future mirror his failed past? He slumped in his chair. Maybe that was the way things were meant to be.

5

Perry's Camera, Tustin

The next day Marcus walked into Perry's Camera, the area's preeminent studio store, across the street and down the block from the studio.

"So, uh, you're the new guy? The MB-whatever?" an old hippie asked slowly.

"And I bet you're Perry, right?" Ramsay said. He had heard rumors of Perry's past.

"Yeah, man. Perry Hobek." They shook hands using the peace grip, palm-to-palm.

Ramsay felt like he had just time-traveled to the sixties. Perry's grubby appearance and facial hair were subordinate only to the prominence of his bloodshot eyes and slurred voice.

"I'm Marcus Ramsay. Nice to meet you," Ramsay said. "The word's out, I guess. The MBA?"

"Yeah, man. You look like a damn suit!" Perry pushed Ramsay's shoulder.

Ramsay laughed.

"I hear you do some pretty fancy shooting in the dark," Perry said.

"Doesn't anybody else around here do light painting?" Ramsay asked.

"No. most of 'em use Chimera light boxes or huge homemade ones. Have for years."

"That leaves me alone, I guess."

"You could say that," Hobek said. "By the way, I sent some assistants looking for work over to your place. My place is sort of the center of the photo biz around south Orange County. If you need any help, call."

"Hey, Perry, thanks for getting the account opened so fast."

"My pleasure, man," Perry said. "By the way, looks like you got a bunch of charges on it already." He held out a small batch of invoices.

Ramsay looked at the signatures on the invoices. "Wait. These are all signed by a person I don't even know," Ramsay said.

"Sorry. 'Fraid you're responsible. That is, unless you tell us in advance which signatures are okay and which aren't."

"Hmm, I guess I understand. I'll go back and straighten this out. Give you a call," Ramsay said, and walked out. He climbed into his Jeep for the drive to SMS Advertising for a presentation of his portfolio.

As he drove down Red Hill Avenue, he thought about how funny it was that he had heard about Perry and Perry knew all about him. Like in a small town, the word had spread through Orange County photo circles that an MBA had opened shop and was using a light painting technique.

And what about those charges on his Perry's account?

After the portfolio presentation, Ramsay returned to his studio. He pulled up, got out of his car, and approached an anxious-looking Hispanic fellow, about thirty-five, who paced back and forth outside the suite.

"Can I help you with something?" Marcus asked.

"Hi. You Ramsay?" the man asked. "I'm Tyler Gonzales. Perry sent me over." He offered a card.

"That's me. Perry said he'd send people over."

They entered Ramsay's door.

"Boy, these are great shots," Tyler said as they wandered through Ramsay's client lounge.

"It's a shame the local art directors don't think so." Ramsay opened the studio door, explaining how he had just had a frustrating portfolio presentation at SMS.

Tyler was husky and self-conscious, with dark eyes, black bushy hair, and an undersized mouth sitting on a puffy pockmarked face. "Why'd they hate 'em? Your work is so cool."

"I'm glad someone likes the stuff. I've worked hard at it. But over at SMS they said their clients wouldn't appreciate the style—too arty."

"How'd you learn how to do this?"

"Taught myself in Texas," Ramsay said. Marcus explained that, even before he had left his corporate job, he had built a little studio in his garage and practiced his photography for hours. He used countless four-by-five Polaroids, always taking meticulous notes in order to learn as quickly as possible. He tried one lighting approach, then shot a Polaroid to see if his idea had worked. Then he shot another, then another. It was expensive but effective.

Ramsay explained how, out of nowhere, he had gotten fired and suddenly had all the time in the world to devote to his photography. He had methodically recorded details of each exposure on every Polaroid print: shutter speed, aperture (f-stop), how many seconds his new fiber-optic painting device was employed, and on what facet of the subject.

Marcus explained to Tyler how he felt guilty for not being the primary wage earner at home. "Kathy treated me like I had let her down. I'd get all excited about the new lighting, but she'd just yawn. Hardly supportive."

"Not good."

"She hated that I wasn't the corporate guy anymore. She'd have these phone calls with her dad. He always supported the anti-Marcus thinking."

"Teaming up on you?"

"I guess I can't blame the guy. He wanted me to stay the perfect guy his daughter married."

"Then it took you a couple of years to learn this style?"

"Actually, a year. I was obsessed with it. I guess it helped me counteract my failure in the corporate world."

"Bev—she's my wife—is really supportive," Gonzales said. "I think I might have a chance in this photo business, but my shooting isn't anywhere near yours."

"Just takes time and practice."

"So, how'd you end up in Orange County?"

"Kathy took a director of marketing job at Pepe's Café headquarters over in Irvine. I decided to go for it and open a studio. So, we moved out here."

"Just like that?"

"Not quite. The firing and move were tough on our marriage, so we separated for a few months. Then, lo and behold, she had me served with papers yesterday."

"Out of the blue?"

Ramsay nodded. "Yeah. I thought we were about to get back together, too."

"Hey, I'm sorry."

"It's okay," Ramsay said. "I should've seen it coming."

"Well, I really think your work is something special," Tyler said. "You even ought to teach this technique. I bet a lot of guys would love to learn it. Around here, all they do is boring lighting—pretty bad, if you ask me."

Ramsay laughed at the way Tyler said it.

"Really, I'm not kidding." As they talked, Gonzales helped Ramsay set up a few studio lights.

Ramsay pulled out a small black metal box on wheels with an attached six-foot-long, half-inch-wide hose. "It's called a *Hosemaster*," Ramsay said. "Fiber optics."

"Cool. I've heard about it but never seen one."

Ramsay explained how to use the device, in particular how to perform multiple exposures to render a faint dark line around subjects and how to mix sharp and soft-focus, like Renoir did in his paintings.

"So, that's how you make it look like that? It doesn't even look like a photograph."

"Basically. Cool, huh?" Ramsay said. "Takes a lot of practice."

"I'd say. Perry says you need an assistant or manager. Any chance I could apply?"

"Maybe I could hire you freelance for some assignments. I'm not sure if I need a full-timer yet."

"Is it true that you have an MBA?"

"Yeah, marketing. Why?"

"Smarty, huh? Well, I think you got something going with this light painting stuff. Bev would love it."

"Thanks. You said you were a cop?" Ramsay asked.

"Twenty years. Compton force."

"We're both switching careers. You were a cop; I was a suit."

"Bev couldn't take the violence anymore," Gonzales said. "Especially when I lost my partner two months ago—after seven years."

"I'm so sorry," Ramsay said.

They continued talking until a large, attractive woman, maybe thirty, walked in. Her hands were stuffed in her pockets, and she wore a baggy white T-shirt. Her eyes sparkled, and she announced herself in a loud, clear voice: "Hi there. I'm Rita. Rita Scorpino? The guys at Perry's told me about the Chicago shooter starting up over here. That you?" she asked.

"Sure is," Ramsay said. "Marcus Ramsay." He extended his hand; she shook it.

"I grew up back there, too," she said. "Looking for a regular gig." She chortled between her bullet sentences, adding a levity to her demeanor. "I'm from Elk Grove Village."

"Really? I'm from Morton Grove," Ramsay said.

"Close," she laughed.

Tyler appeared overwhelmed by her outspokenness and shuffled away. He apologized, saying he had to pick up his son, Jeffrey, from school.

"Hey, see you, Tyler," Ramsay called. "Nice meeting you."

Tyler waved back, looking at Scorpino, and closed the studio door.

Rita continued, "So I came out fifteen years ago, had a daughter, and worked at a legal firm for a while. Then I decided to give photography a go," she said.

"I guess most photographers do something else first," Ramsay said.

"So, over at Perry's they said you were in some corporation?"

"Yeah, marketing at Puritan—first in Chicago, then at one of their divisions in Texas," he said. "Then I left—not my choice."

"Too bad," she said. "I was controller at the legal firm."

"Big job?"

"Right. Then I asked for a raise when everyone else got one."

"And?"

"They gave me a pink slip."

"You're kidding?" he said and shook his head. "That figures."

"Yeah; they weren't dealing straight with me," she said.

"Well, I haven't met any straightforward lawyers yet, but I hear there's a lot of hustlers and trash out here on the Coast," Ramsay said. "You can't trust anyone."

"True." She fidgeted. "Everybody's looking for an angle."

"We've gone through similar shit, you and I," he said.

"No josh."

The sturdy woman was masculine in her demeanor, twenty pounds overweight, and articulate for an assistant photographer.

Ramsay liked her voice—clear as a bell, a bit singsongy. She spoke of multiple trips she had made to Escalen at Big Sur—up the California coast—and described the hot mineral baths, great massages, and seminars they had there. She described the peacefulness she felt after each trip and suggested Ramsay go.

"Sounds cool," he said. Ramsay could tell Rita was a feelings-type person, not driven by to-do lists.

"That's me." Rita shrugged and went on, telling him about her family.

Rita didn't look like she could've possibly given birth

to a girl who was now a teenager. She was smart, Ramsay guessed, but talked with a mixture of sophisticated talk and a simple vocabulary.

"It must have been tough getting booted out of the legal firm so arbitrarily." Ramsay recalled his own banishment from corporate America.

"Those fucking pinstriped assholes," she said all of a sudden.

Ramsay faced her suddenly. "What?"

"Oh, sorry," she said. "I guess calling a spade a spade is a Midwest thing; at least it's *my* thing."

"Mine, too," Ramsay said.

"You know, you really do nice work, Marcus." She pointed toward the client lounge.

"With a little luck, it'll catch on with clients."

"Do you really turn off all the lights, open the lens, and use fiber-optic light?" She rocked forward and backward on her feet, pointing to the camera.

"Yeah," he said. "I just apply the fiber-optic light over a long exposure in near-darkness with a small aperture like $F22^{1/2}$. I sometimes use flashlights and penlights, and correct their color temperature with CC filters."

"I've heard of that Hosemaster." She pointed to it. "First one I've seen. Funny name. Aaron Jones invented it, right?"

"Right."

"This is a super studio, Marcus," she said, looking around.

"Three thousand square feet. One thousand office, the rest studio," he said proudly.

"Cool." Her laugh echoed. "Yours is a better shape than most of the ones I've seen around—nice and wide.

Most of 'em are like bowling alleys."

They kept talking. Ramsay liked Rita Scorpino and, from all appearances, she liked him.

The next day, when Ramsay arrived at the studio, Rita stood out front gabbing with two police officers who had parked their patrol cars diagonal to the studio door.

"So, what gives?" Marcus called as he walked across the lot toward them.

"Break-in," she said. There was glass on the ground in front of the shattered door.

"Shit!" he said.

"Are you the owner?" one policeman said.

"Yes, Officer."

"Miss Scorpino work for you?"

"Almost, I guess."

"Well, she called this in," he said.

"Looks like I owe you one, Rita," Ramsay said. "Anything missing?"

"Not as far as I can tell, but you should look around."

"I will."

After they answered questions for the police report, Marcus and Rita crunched over the glass into the suite. They walked through the client lounge into Ramsay's office.

"Say, Rita, I appreciate the help. But before we can make your employment official, I need to know a few things."

"What things?" she asked defensively.

"Hey, easy," Ramsay said. He stowed his worn attaché by the side of his desk and sat down, leaving her standing.

"Well?" she said, and fumbled with her belt.

"The living with your parents bit. What gives with that?"

"Well . . ." Scorpino rocked back and forth. Her voice suddenly sounded like a baby's. "I guess I should've said something. I had this ugly divorce. I've been trying to get over it."

"Sorry."

She sighed. "My ex ran with the wrong crowd. He fixed Harleys and sold drugs. Got me mixed up with all of that stuff, the asshole. I even used for a few years. We were always running from the law."

"Cocaine?" he asked.

"Yeah. Smack, too."

"Jeez." Ramsay cringed. "Heavy stuff."

"But since then, I've cleaned up and started over. Honest."

"Really? Can I ask, do you have a record?"

"Uh, no."

"How long since the divorce?"

"Two years."

"You doing all right now?"

"Yeah. Got a boyfriend, Harvey. He's a little obsessed with me, but other than that, he's okay." She laughed. "I gained a bunch of weight when I went clean. Then I moved in with my folks; they helped me a lot with Brandy."

"What about the legal firm?"

"They heard about the past stuff and fired me, so I started assisting for some shooters around here—just to get my feet wet. You can call any of 'em if you need a reference."

"You said you were the controller at the legal firm," Ramsay said. "But you don't have the education or experience to be a real controller."

"Well, they called it that. I was a glorified office manager and did payroll. The girls sort of reported to me, especially when the partners wanted somebody fired. When the girls started to treat me like their leader, the partners didn't dig that."

"And?"

"That's when they cut me loose." Scorpino stood there kicking the floor like a little kid. "I'm sorry I didn't explain all that, Marcus. I'm still trying to shake loose of it, you know? Harvey thinks I should be more pissed at those lawyer assholes."

"Thanks for filling me in. I'm going through my own divorce. It's just starting to sink in."

"Then you must know a little how I'm feeling." Her big eyes teared, and her lower lip quivered.

"Yeah," he said. "She hit me with the papers a few days ago."

"How long were you married?"

"Ten years."

"Wow," she said.

"I think we grew apart the last few, you know?"

"Too bad."

"I became the bad guy because I wanted to follow my dreams after I got rejected by the hallowed corporation. So, she filed—just like that."

"Sudden?"

"Yeah, after we had this nice dinner, too. I thought we were on the verge of getting back together—right."

Just then a nasal female voice called from the front door, "Hello, anyone!"

"Excuse me for a second, Rita." Ramsay rose and

walked out of his office, toward the voice.

"What's all this mess?" a scrawny young woman asked as she carefully stepped over the glass shards in the reception area.

"Careful," Ramsay said. "Can I help you?"

"Checking in for the Backman shoot tomorrow."

"What about it?" he asked.

"I'm the talent."

"The hand model?"

"Well, that's what you ordered, right?"

He nodded. Ramsay thought she didn't look like a model. He was already getting nervous about his first shoot with Amy Baker, the so-called art director from hell. Now this grubby-looking model appears?

"I'm Jessica," she said. "Jessica Dasher. Nancy sent me over so you could check out the hands. Just call me Jesse." In her mid-twenties, Jessica wore a faded sleeveless blouse, torn jeans, and old sandals. She tiptoed like a wobbly flamingo on the broken glass, obviously trying to find the right place to stand as Rita started to sweep up around her.

All Ramsay could picture was Jessica cutting her feet and the frivolous lawsuits that might ensue.

"I guess I don't really look like a model, do I?" she asked. She studied the departing police cars, then danced around the glass shards and Rita's broom. "I'm sorry. I'm so clumsy."

"We better go into my office before you get cut," Ramsay said, slightly irritated. She had scraggly brown hair, a long nose, a skinny frame, a peach fuzz mustache, large undefined lips, and beady eyes—not exactly Cheryl Tiegs or Cybill Shepherd.

They walked into his office and remained standing.

He turned to her. "Well, let's look at your hands."

She foisted them at him matter-of-factly, hanging them in the air, bent at the wrists. "Here."

Ramsay flinched. They were soft-looking, uniformly colored, and perfectly proportioned, her delicate fingers slender and just a breath longer than the span across each palm, creating a gracefulness in their line. Each of her nails was a glowing pink oval, painted with crystal clear polish, revealing skin underneath each one—ideal hands for high-tech shots. Nancy Burret, the head of one of the local modeling agencies, had done well when she picked Jessica.

"Your hands are beautiful, Jesse," Ramsay said.

"Now I suppose you want to see my book," she said with a pout. She laid her portfolio on his desk and flipped through ten or so photographs, amateurly taken, each failing to do her hands justice. Ramsay studied them carefully.

"This is it?"

"I knew you'd have a problem with them," she whined.

"Jessica, sit down, okay?"

"Something wrong, Mr. Ramsay?"

"Just call me Marcus."

"OK, Marcus."

"Let me offer you a little advice, if I may," he said.

"I'd be honored."

"Let's not overdo it, Jessica. Your hands are beautiful, but your book—which is supposed to help get you the jobs—doesn't do them justice. Why don't we shoot a couple of outtakes for your portfolio during the Backman job tomorrow? What do you think?"

"For my promo card? Would you mind, Mr. Ramsay? Marcus?"

"No problem." Ramsay was a bit taken back by the idolatry in her tone. "Also, let me say this, for what it's worth."

"Oh, anything, anything," she said.

"To make it in this business, a model should come off like a model. Even if you only model your hands, you need to present a professional image for the client. In this case Amy Baker is Backman's art director, one of the toughest around. So, you have to be thinking nice outfit, nice hair, nice makeup—the whole bit."

"Whatever you want, Marcus. Really." Jessica blushed and looked down. Then she looked up and spoke in a confident voice: "Marcus, I'm an actress, too. I can be whoever you need me to be."

"Fine. It's only advice," he said.

"I appreciate it, Marcus. I felt privileged to get this job." She blushed.

"Privileged?" he said. *That's a first,* Ramsay thought. "I'm new around here. And I was just trying to help with my comments, Jesse."

"But I feel so special that you'd give me all this advice," she said.

"They were just a few professional comments."

"Now you're discounting what you said," she said. Her brows perched.

"What is it?" he asked. "What'd I say?"

"They always hated us Dasher twins because we were loaded and my dad owned his own company."

"What's that have to do with anything?"

"Now I'm just a struggling actress and model. Dad's disowned me for shipping off to the Coast instead of going to Harvard or getting my CPA. But he'll always love my twin sister, the park ranger, goddess of nature."

Jessica was acting weird, Ramsay thought. At least she didn't call her father Daddy like Kathy did.

"I'm really struggling for the first time in my life," she said. "It's plenty hard, you know?"

"I'm sure. It must be tough being an actress," he said.

"Yada, yada, yada. My big deal was an intro to *Seinfeld*—duh. You would've hated it. Took an afternoon. Big deal."

He was nonplussed by her chatter. "That's impressive. Honest."

"An intro? For only one episode?" she snickered. "Big deal."

"Still—"

"I can tell you're not really impressed," she said. "You're just bullshitting me."

"Wait," he said. "Really, Jessica, I think you have tons of potential, especially with your hands."

"Sure. That's what they all say," she said, pouting. She reached in her pockets and pulled a stash of rings out. She ceremonially put one on each finger.

"Be careful not to mar those pretty hands," he said.

"No problem." She smiled, then threw him a scornful look. "Listen, Mr. Ramsay, or Marcus, whatever. Don't you think I know how to be careful with my hands?"

He cleared his throat. "Sure. Listen, your hands are perfect for these high-tech ads. We don't have to argue about anything."

She became innocent and demure. "You really like them?" She swirled her hands in the air. "Not just for tech shots, though, right?"

"I guess, sure," he said. "You're right. I should've mentioned that, but I've been a little preoccupied with my divorce."

"You're getting divorced?" she moaned like a put-out teen. "That's so-o-o sad."

"I'm in the process," he said.

"I hope I didn't upset you," she said. "I know I upset you. But maybe you should write down your home number and I can make it up to you, okay? I can call you sometime and we could get together for a swim and pizza. It'll do you good." She handed him a business card and pen; he wrote his number.

By the time Jessica putted away in her Geo Metro minutes later, Marcus Ramsay's head spun from her jabbering. Her rapid-fire bickering was mixed with a deferential worship that made him feel good, but a bit overwhelmed. There was a bubble of neurosis encompassing her entire persona.

That afternoon about two, Tyler Gonzales walked past Rita as she went about her tasks at the desk in the reception area. Tyler was about to go into the studio just as Ramsay poked his head out of the studio door. "Oh, hi, Tyler. What's up?" Ramsay asked.

"Hey, Marcus," he said as he backed into the client lounge and pointed at the reception area. "So, you picked somebody else? A full-timer?"

Ramsay shrugged. "Immediate chemistry."

Tyler sighed audibly and gabbed how the weather would be perfect for diving that weekend.

Ramsay interrupted him, "Don't worry, Tyler. I can still hire you freelance."

"Sure." Tyler's little smile strained. He made an awkward excuse and looked at his clunky watch, like he suddenly remembered an appointment. He started to back away.

"Honest," Ramsay said. "In fact, I'm shooting Backman tomorrow and need a second assistant. You free?"

"Really?" he asked.

"Eight o'clock?"

"I'll be here." Tyler left the studio whistling, but stopped and turned away as he passed Rita. Marcus imagined from his demeanor that Tyler had already told his family that an opportunity at the studio was locked in.

"Well, I suppose I wouldn't have to use Jessica again," Ramsay said later to Rita, having sensed her disapproval of the hand model. "Maybe she is sort of quirky."

"She seems smart, I'll give you that," Rita said. "But I don't know if having a crazy hand model is what you want for your first big shoot. I'd honestly trust her only as far as I could throw her."

"Really?" Ramsay said.

"Well, it's sort of shocking, what she said on her way out. She didn't see me in the front office when she walked by . . . or she just didn't care."

"What did she say?" he asked.

"'Fucking know-it-all,'" Rita said.

Ramsay winced.

Off and on for the next several hours Ramsay wondered about Jessica's odd comment. He really had thought she liked him, even respected him.

Marcus appreciated Rita's assessment of Jessica. Rita reminded him of Kathy, the way she seemed capable of great dispassion. It would be good to have a truly objective person on his team, he thought.

Later that afternoon, Rita stood at his office door.

"Let's get going." She signaled toward the front door as the prerecorded dinner bugle sounded at the marine base next to the business park.

"Where are we going?"

"The SIP meeting. The Society of Illustrative Photographers? Over at James Honeybear's studio on Main in Santa Ana. I told you about it at lunch."

"Right. Oh, Rita?" Ramsay asked as he rose.

"What?" She turned around.

"Thanks for keeping an eye out for me," he said. "You know, Jessica's weird comment."

"Oh." She smiled. "It's nothing. That's why you hired me."

The walls of Honeybear's studio were covered with zolotone, an artificial granite effect made with a special kind of spray paint. Around James's studio, everything was the best: the Sinar Bron P1 camera, the latest Bron-Color lighting equipment, and a kitchen area with a granite preparation surface. Shooting food was James Honeybear's specialty.

Like a well-honed politician, Stan Devlin, the temporary president of SIP, stood near the front door and welcomed members. "How are you? It's been a long time. Nice to see you." Ramsay walked up and Devlin greeted him with two hands. Devlin must've remembered him.

Then Stan turned to Rita and smiled. "Hi, Rita," he said. "How are you? How's Randy?"

Ramsay and Rita took name tags from the table nearby, filled them out, and affixed them to their T-shirts.

"You know Stan?" Ramsay asked her. "Who's Randy?"

Scorpino blushed. "Well, back in Elk Grove, Stan

knew my brother Randy. Stan's originally from there. How do *you* know him?"

"Stan was the first shooter I met in Orange County," Ramsay said. "He gave me a few pointers about finishing my studio. Why didn't you mention you knew him?"

"Didn't come up. That a big deal?" she asked.

"Not really," Ramsay said.

"Hey, everyone take your seats!" Art Zipper squealed into the microphone.

The mingling group of fifty took their seats. The more you were "known" by the group, the farther forward you positioned your seat. The less recognizable the name on your adhesive name tag, the farther back you sat—a caste system of sorts. Soon the group rumbled to silence.

Stan Devlin walked up to the mike like a portly king. "Last time we didn't finish talking rates...," he said importantly to the group, and cleared his throat. Through the array of bodies, he looked directly at Ramsay. "We have to keep charging high enough...," he said.

"Like you fellows?" A shooter with a proper-sounding foreign accent stood in the semidark and pointed to the senior photographers in front. "If we charged what you fellows do, no one would hire us."

"But, Chester," Devlin answered, "we're all professionals, right? We all have families, overhead, and advertising. We should all be charging at least fifteen hundred dollars a day."

"Fifteen hundred dollars?" Chester repeated. "I'll never get any work!"

"Chester, you must..." By the end of Devlin's droning lecture, explicitly supporting uniformly high pricing, he appeared to have gained the upper hand.

Then Ramsay raised his hand.

"Yes, Marcus," Devlin said.

"I know I'm new, but I sort of agree with Chester. This pricing approach sounds like a Middle Eastern oil cartel: They try to maximize profits by first agreeing to price the same as one another. It's inevitable that one member will lower his price and win most of the business—that's Economics 101. Won't promote much trust among us; that's for sure."

Chester Major raised his hand. "Chap has a point."

"Interesting, Marcus, but that's not how it works around here. We stick together," Devlin said, and looked at his watch. "Let's break for refreshments."

The group known as the clique, the seven senior shooters, had been sitting in silence except for Stan Devlin and Art Zipper. Now they all quietly talked over their beer. A group of the lesser-knowns, who were physically excluded from the clique by two rows of chairs, gathered together and talked.

"You know," Chester Major said in his South African accent, "I would go to SIP meetings more often, but those fellows aren't very friendly. After each meeting I go back to my studio and struggle to do what Devlin says, but it never works. He's a union dickhead. If you ask me, they're all union dickheads."

"I don't get it," Ramsay said. "What's the big deal? It's a free country. You can price any way you want. They don't have any power over you."

"But Devlin talks like we'd be committing some sort of crime," Major said. "He'd probably call us to task in front of the whole group if he ever found out we didn't price as high as he says."

"If you ask me, they're just throwing their weight around," Ramsay said.

"Maybe so. But the clique's been together for years," Chester said, "and they resent new shooters and their ideas."

"Why do they keep to themselves like that?" Ramsay asked as he eyed the clique. At that moment, he noticed Stan Devlin's and the other heads turn in his direction.

"They're arrogant," Chester said. "Look at them staring over here."

"I presume their studios are doing well?" Ramsay said.

"You'd think that by the way they act. They supposedly all charge fifteen-hundred a day."

Ramsay turned to Rita. "What's your take on it, Rita? You've been around here a little bit."

"Oh, I don't know. They treat me okay when I assist for them," she said. "I was even Stan's studio manager for a short time. He's okay."

"Maybe they treat you okay because you're a woman, but they act cool to us," Chester said.

"They don't seem very gifted in the social graces; I'll give you that," Ramsay said.

"I'd say!" Chester laughed.

"Oh, they're not that bad, Chester," Rita said. "You're making a big deal about this. Marcus was acting like a know-it-all with that economics stuff—letting his MBA show."

"That so, Rita?" Ramsay said, and sipped his beer. He eyed the clique, hovering together. "I didn't realize I told you about my MBA."

"Oh?" She flinched. "Didn't you? I think you did."

"Say, Marcus. I heard you've had some break-ins at your place," Chester said. "Buggers."

"Yeah."

"Santa Ana scum, I bet," Major said.

"Could be. The front door was bashed in; the glass was everywhere. No other loss. We weren't shooting that day."

"Thank goodness for small miracles," Major said.

That night at home Ramsay worried about his Backman shoot the following day. Would Jessica blow it for him? Would she piss off his new client, Amy Baker, known to Orange County photographers as a particularly tough art director?

He dialed Nancy Burret, Jessica's modeling agent, to see if she might be working late. Maybe he could find out if Jessica had any problems with clients in the past. He felt relieved when he got Nancy's answering machine. It would be better if he didn't know about Jessica's past, he thought. After all, except for the strange comment she made at the end of her visit and the fact that she seemed to like to argue, Jessica had made him feel good, the way she kissed up to him, even if she got a little carried away.

Ramsay lay in bed, hoping that his shoot would go well and Jessica wouldn't do anything to spoil it.

As he became drowsy, his thoughts drifted to Kathy and how she'd be surprised that he was already shooting a big assignment. Ramsay smiled in the dark. Starting tomorrow, his new life would begin to nullify the lingering pain he felt from his old one.

6

Marcus Ramsay Photographic

Just after dawn the next day, Ramsay drove down Red Hill Avenue toward the studio. Now that he had hired Rita, he felt a sense of peace for the first time in weeks, like maybe things were fitting together in his new life. And Tyler seemed like an eager, supportive assistant, too. Maybe this first big shoot for Backman would be phenomenal.

When Ramsay turned the corner into his business park, he felt like he had been kicked in the gut. There was all sorts of activity in front of his suite: a police car, some kind of security car, red and blue blinking lights, and a crowd of uniformed bodies. He sped to the front door and jumped out of his Jeep. Glass was scattered at the entrance and throughout his reception area.

"Again?" he complained to a policeman. Ramsay fumed as he surveyed the damage.

"You Marcus Ramsay?" the cop asked.

"This is the second time this has happened!" Ramsay said.

"Just calm down, sir."

"Well, I have my first big shoot today. It's not a good day for this bullshit."

"Calm down. Let's fill out a report," the cop said. "This happened before?"

"Day before yesterday."

"What happened?" Donald asked as he waddled over from Sycamore Studios.

"It's another damn break-in."

Donald shook his head. "Too bad, son."

"You have any enemies, Mr. Ramsay?" the officer asked.

"I just opened for business!" Ramsay said. "How could I have any enemies?"

"I do have some good news, Marcus," Donald said. "Looks like you could use some right now. My cousin's an artist's rep, up north of LA."

"So?"

"She said she'd take a look at your portfolio. She'll call you."

Ramsay shook his head. "Maybe that'll help me pay for all this repair."

"Her name is Vanessa Franklin. Swell gal."

"I wonder if I even should've done this photo thing," Ramsay said.

"Marcus, don't start doubting yourself!" McKenzie slapped Ramsay on the back. "You'll be okay."

Just then Rita pulled up with a crazed-looking man with long, wild hair. They got out of the car.

"What happened?" she asked.

"Again," Ramsay moaned. "They did it again."

"Man, this is awful. Especially today. Oh, by the way, Marcus, this is my boyfriend, Harvey."

The long-haired man extended his hand through the car window and mumbled greetings. "How ya doing? Rita told me about you."

"She mentioned you, too."

"Listen, you take good care of her," he whispered in a threatening tone as he pushed back his hair, then adjusted a knife in a sheath on his belt. "Ya hear?"

"Harvey!" Rita said. She punched him in the shoulder as the police climbed into their cars. "I gotta get to work now."

He leaned up and kissed her hard on the lips. Then he turned on the car's ignition and drove away, looking back twice at Ramsay and the police.

"Sorry about that," she said. "I told you Harvey was a little intense."

"I'll say."

A few minutes later, as the police pulled away, Ramsay sipped on his first cup of tea as Rita swept up the glass. The prerecorded reveille sounded at the marine base as he walked back to his office. Even though he was shaken by the break-in, his first big shoot with Amy Baker would finally give him an opportunity to use his light painting expertise, the only thing he felt confident about.

The front doorbell rang.

Seconds later a trim, attractive woman glided into his office. "Hi," she said softly.

He rubbed his eyes. "Jessica! Is that you? Jessica Dasher?"

She was dressed in an attractive floor-length peasant dress with a delicate floral pattern and empire waist. Her hair was pulled back with intricate tortoiseshell combs. A large gold hoop earring dangled from each ear. Her cheeks blushed mauve. Her eye makeup was scant. Her lips were rosy and perfectly formed. Her peach fuzz mustache was gone, her smile glowed, and her pasty complexion had been transformed into smooth, lightly tanned skin.

"Surprised?" she asked. "You like what you see?"

"I'm impressed."

She smiled. "I knew this is what you'd want."

"It's a significant change from yesterday. Very professional. How'd you do it?"

"I am an actress, you know." She smiled. "I thought you'd approve."

"You look like it."

"I can be whoever you want me to be, Marcus," she said and flashed another smile.

"Like a chameleon, I'd say. Want to grab some tea before the client gets here?"

"That would be perfect." Jessica followed him to the studio kitchen.

They drank tea until the Backman Medical personnel—more people than necessary—poured into the studio to supervise the dramatic shot. The line was led by Amy Baker, who marched in like she owned the place. "Well, I guess we can start now," her voice echoed through the studio.

"Good morning, Amy," Ramsay said. "Coffee?"

She nodded, then waited to be served.

First the high-tech set was built. After the camera and lighting equipment were positioned, Rita and Tyler helped Ramsay apply his light painting technique. Ramsay set the oxygenator, Backman's new product, on the grid to enhance the technical quality of the shot. The studio lights were dimmed and the camera set on "T" or "time exposure." An underexposed "base" of light, with a diffusion filter over the lens, was applied. The filter was removed. Next, for the so-called "detail" exposure, Ramsay waved his fiber-optic wand in near-dark ten inches from the product, lighting specific areas to enhance its attributes. By noon, many Polaroids had been taken to optimize the lighting. Amy seemed to like the progress the shoot was taking.

"Okay. Let's break for lunch," Ramsay said. "We'll go across the street to the Barn Restaurant."

As Tyler and Rita chatted with Amy Baker on their way out of the studio, Jessica Dasher straggled behind, swishing her peasant dress. "I think I'll just eat my yogurt here, Marcus," she said. "That okay?"

"Sure. That's fine, Jessica. It's been a tough shoot," he said.

"Phew." A few strands of hair dangled out of place.

"Just relax in my office. You've done a great job."

"It's important for me to ace this one."

"You will. You can take a couple of outtakes of the shot for your portfolio."

"I appreciate your faith in me," she said. "I feel like I'm a real part of your team."

"You are. Hey, see you later." Marcus ran to catch up with the group.

When they returned an hour later, Ramsay was annoyed. During lunch, Rita had teased about how *she* was undoubtedly the reason Marcus Ramsay Photographic would become a pervasive force in Orange County advertising photography.

As the shoot progressed, Rita cracked joke after joke, each of which found Amy's funny bone. "So, how many photographers does it take to shoot one four-by-five sheet of film?" Rita asked.

Irritated, Ramsay finally interrupted. "Excuse me. We

need to measure the bellows factor before we can shoot the final film."

Rita went to the workbench to get the bellows factor measuring device. "I can't find it," she said.

"I left it right on the pegboard!" Ramsay said. "Do you need my help?"

"No. it's not here, Marcus," Tyler called.

They scoured the studio, opening drawers and clanging equipment, but the bellows factor device couldn't be found.

"Is there a problem?" Amy Baker said impatiently. "I hope I'm not paying for this." She looked at her watch. "And I have a meeting at the office."

Ramsay flushed. "One of you go over to Perry's and buy another one."

"I'll go. I know my way around there," Rita said.

"Just put it on my account," he grumbled.

"I hope I'm not paying for a new one of those doomaflotchies." Amy crunched her nose. She raised her eyebrows at Rita as she left.

Holding her pose perfectly, Jessica Dasher hummed.

"You hanging in there?" Ramsay asked.

She nodded and smiled. "You're sure I'm doing a good job?" she whispered.

"Until a minute ago, this whole shoot was going well," he said.

Minutes later Rita walked back into the studio with a new bellows device. "To the rescue!"

"Let's continue," Ramsay said.

"Marcus, is this okay?" Jessica asked, this time in a provocative tone. Ramsay was surprised at her manner. The way she said it, he wasn't sure if she was referring to how she looked or how she was positioning her hands around the product.

"Uh, sure. We'll get some good takes from this, Jessica," he said and cleared his throat.

The studio was darkened; the Hosemaster was turned on. Ramsay waved it over the oxygenator.

"Whoops. I think I moved my hand on that take," she said.

"That's okay. We'll get it on the next one."

"Sure?" she whispered. "Is this right?"

"Great."

As she posed carefully, Ramsay noticed through the dim light that she glanced at him longingly. After several minutes, Ramsay thought he saw a flirtatious little grin.

After the shoot, they were waiting the hour and a half it took for the final film to be processed at Datachrome. Marcus asked Jessica to follow him to his office.

"Well? How did it go, Marcus?" she asked.

"I think they'll be great."

"Wonderful!" she said.

"You can take some of the outtakes for your book."

"What did you want to talk to me about?"

"Jessica, it looked like you were looking at me . . . well, a little provocatively. It sort of distracted me."

"Excuse me?" she asked.

"It sure looked like it—your eyes, your mouth."

"Well, maybe a little," she said, and smiled.

"I thought so. Just ease up on the suggestive stuff, okay?"

"Well, I was hoping we might get together sometime," she said. "There's a great pool at my apartment, north of LA. I told you about it. We could go for a swim, then pizza after. Sound good?"

"I happen to be headed up near there to see a photo rep tomorrow."

"Super. Is it a plan, then?"

"Hmm, sure, I guess," he said. "But with the divorce being so recent, I haven't dated a lot, so—"

"Come on; it'll be good for you. I'll call you later."

Minutes later, after Ramsay reviewed the processed film, Amy Baker and the rest of her crew left the studio in a clump, talking among themselves.

"The film looks great, Marcus!" she called. "Send me an invoice."

"Will do," he said.

"I'll definitely be calling you again. These shots are wonderful. Good job, Jessica."

"Thank you," she called.

Tyler appeared at the office door. "All cleaned up back there, boss. Want to get a beer?"

"No thanks, Tyler. Maybe another night," Ramsay said. "Send me an invoice for today's shoot, okay? See you."

"Aye-aye," Tyler saluted and walked out.

Darkness descended upon the Cole Business Park.

Jessica slipped out behind Tyler, waving good-bye. As Ramsay listened to her putt away, he pondered their impending date.

Rita walked in.

"Boy that's sort of a surprise," Ramsay said.

"What?"

"Jessica."

"What about her?" she asked.

"She asked me out for tomorrow night."

"No offense, but she's sort of spooky, if you ask me."

"You're just jealous," he joshed. "You know, Rita, I don't know where this vandalism bullshit is coming from, but it can't continue."

"No kidding."

"The police told me they'd need to start charging for any special treatment they give me if this prank bit becomes a regular deal. I can't afford that, plus the cost of the repair."

"Rip-off," she said.

"Those are just the rules in Tustin. Oh, and at Perry's? They said I had charges against my account dated two days ago that I never made. They were approved by some strange signature. You know anything about that?"

"Uh . . . no."

He swung around in his desk chair. "And I don't want to spend money every time we can't find the damn bellows comp device. That's twenty bucks down the drain."

"All right, all right," she said. "Ease up."

"Well, it seems that we suddenly have a lot of extra expenses."

"I'll check on them in the morning."

"It just pisses me off," he said. "Part of your job is to keep a handle on this stuff."

"Don't get pissed," she said. "I just started."

Early the next evening Ramsay met James Honeybear at the Barn for a drink. The place looked like a huge barn inside: rustic table and chairs, rough-hewn rafters, and exposed wood walls.

"How did the shoot go yesterday?" Honeybear asked as he walked up, pulled back a chair, and sat his lineman's frame down.

"Super," Ramsay said. "Amy Baker liked the film."

"Good. Good." Honeybear nodded his large head.

"So, you played football?" Ramsay asked.

"High school, some college."

"What position?"

"Offensive tackle. Junior year I busted up my knees pretty bad."

"And picked up a camera?"

"Yeah. Went to Brooks after college."

"Brooks?"

"Good photo school up in Santa Barbara."

Their waitress walked up, and they ordered beers.

"So, you think I pissed off the other guys at the last SIP meeting when I put down price fixing?"

"Mostly Stan, but a bunch of the rest of us think you ought to run for office. Elections are coming up."

"I'm not really established yet. Besides, it would take too much time."

"You're computerized at your place, aren't you?" Honeybear asked.

"Yeah."

"You could make it work, then. Do you really have an MBA?" He sipped more beer.

"Yeah. What's the big deal?"

"Sort of unique for a shooter."

"Why, you have your degree plus photo school."

"They give me a hard time about the BA, too," Honeybear said. "Most guys only went to photo school."

Ramsay laughed. "So, they give anyone different a hard time?"

"Especially an MBA. How's your biz going?" Honeybear asked.

"Pretty good. Soon I'm meeting a rep up in LA."
"Who?"
"Vanessa Franklin."
"Heard of her." Honeybear stretched and yawned.
"Maybe she can help," Ramsay said.
"Reps are okay, I guess," Honeybear said.
"You don't sound enthused."
"They take twenty-five percent of everything and don't get you much work. It's like you're subsidizing them, at least for us Orange County shooters. Vanessa's not bad, though. She's got a great accent."
"We'll see," Ramsay said and laughed.
"Say, Marcus?"
"What?"
"You ought to think about running for president of SIP. With that business background of yours, you could probably help us a lot. The organization needs a swift kick."
"You mean it?"
"Sure. You're already getting quite the reputation around here. Might as well leverage it."

Later that night Ramsay surfed channels in his apartment. He really didn't feel much like watching TV. He thought back to when he first got married.

Kathy and he had lived in Chicago and were both struggling with the beginnings of their careers: his at Puritan Corporation; hers, at Standard Brands Systems. Every Sunday they'd drive up Sheridan Road to her folks' house in Highland Park and see their beautiful view of Lake Michigan.

Her father, Arnold Armstrong, was a bulk of a man, bombastic and proud. He had obvious pores that decorated his nose and a voice that was so deep that when he called his diminutive wife, Betty, from the dining room, the crystal in the antique hutch nearby would vibrate.

Betty Armstrong was the source of Kathy's diminutive structure. Betty pranced about on the parquet floors, carrying glasses of iced tea, offering it to her guests with a soft, careful voice.

In those days, Marcus and Kathy spent virtually every Sunday on the Armstrongs' veranda, overlooking the lawn that fell away from the house like a carpet to the lake.

"So, what's next, Marcus?" Arnold had asked him about his career progress one Sunday.

"Arnie, don't talk business now. Let the children relax," Betty said as she set down a plate of cookies.

"The boy's got to make the right moves, Bets," Arnold said. Proud of his advancement at the GBX Corporation, he was now the company's CFO. His rumbling, intimidating voice had undoubtedly helped get him there. "Well, Marcus?"

"They're looking at me for the marketing spot down at the Texas division."

"Wonderful! You hear that, Bets? Our Marcus is on his way."

"Kathy could work at Chips O'Lay, down there in Dallas," Ramsay said.

"You'll have to move?" Bets Armstrong pouted at Marcus and Kathy.

"Mom, it would only be temporary," Kathy said.

"Oh, Bets, we should be happy they're making progress," Arnold said.

Now Marcus Ramsay sat in his puffy easy chair and reflected. He had been fired from that romantic job and lost his idyllic marriage, the cozy in-laws, the iced tea, and the veranda. It was so easy on those Sunday afternoons, when his future seemed a paved road spreading before him.

The road had turned into an overgrown hiking trail and he felt lost. Corporate America had abandoned him; he was struggling to make his new life as smooth as his old one.

Marcus woke up at three in the morning, turned off the TV, and slumped back into his chair, where he dozed fitfully until dawn.

7

Vanessa Franklin's house, Beverly Hills, California
"London? Berlin?" Ramsay said. "Really?"

"Of course, dearie. Your work is beautiful," Vanessa Franklin, a slim, dark-haired, middle-aged Englishwoman, said as she carefully studied each transparency of his portfolio. With poised fingers, she held each image over her tiny light box. "Your lighting is just so . . . other-worldly."

Ramsay explained, "With this light painting technique, I've collapsed the time variable. Each shot takes twenty minutes to shoot or 'paint' in the dark. You would never be able to see this culmination of light at one moment with the naked eye."

"Fascinating," she said. "You really have painted with light, then. Just like Van Gogh or Rembrandt painted with oils!"

He nodded. "I guess."

"Now I understand why you call it light painting," she said.

"Let me think about your proposition for a day or two," he said, and stood. "It was nice meeting you, Vanessa." He extended his hand; she shook it.

Ramsay hurried down the circular staircase in front of Vanessa's Beverly Hills home. As he climbed into his Cherokee, Marcus gazed out at the city-lights view of downtown LA. He drove off to his first post-Kathy date, an evening swim at Jessica's.

As he drove off, Ramsay turned on the radio. He felt satisfied with himself. Vanessa Franklin had loved his work and believed his worldwide marketability was excellent. She even suggested he submit some of his photographs to *Studio Photography* magazine, a prestigious professional publication. "What could they say?" she had said. "'We hate them.'"

"Right." He hadn't really ever thought of his work as that noteworthy, but apparently she felt others would, and she was an artist's rep, so she should know.

Ramsay crept along the Ventura Freeway toward Jessica's place. He got off at the Encino exit and made two quick lefts.

Minutes later, he drove up to 515 Gardner Place. The boring peach-colored, rectangular building had a constant parade of slow-moving older folks, strolling after an early dinner.

He was nervous, thinking about the potential outcomes of his swim with Jessica. He didn't know what to expect of her or what she'd expect of him or if the night would end in some sexual interlude. He thought about how he didn't have any condoms and that would be expected, since AIDS was an issue now, not like when he had dated in the freewheeling early seventies. God, Ramsay hated condoms. He also wondered if their age difference would become an issue. He was in his thirties; she was a decade younger.

He parked his car across the street, jogged to the main entrance, and rang the doorbell for #3F.

"Yes?" a nasal voice answered through the speaker.

"It's me," he said.

"Marcus?" she asked.

"You weren't expecting someone else, were you?"

"Hardly." She laughed. "Come on up."

The doorknob buzzed. He pushed it open and dashed for the slowly closing elevator doors across the lobby. Minutes later, he arrived at the third floor.

"So, how are you?" he said as he walked down the hall toward Jessica's door.

"Perfect." She was leaning on the jamb. As he walked past her, he studied the posters that decorated the walls of her studio apartment. There was a tiny wet bar, two beanbag chairs, and a little TV.

On the built-in bookshelf were paperbacks: Shakespeare, Gore Vidal, Norman Mailer, John Updike—good stuff.

"You don't like them. I can tell," Jessica said. She was dressed in well-washed cut-offs and a T-shirt. No bra.

"What?" he asked.

"The books."

"On the other hand, I'm impressed," he said.

"You're teasing."

"No, really."

She sighed. "When you think about it, Marcus, a home reflects the tastes of the person living there, so over time it becomes a sort of shrine to their existence—a statement about who they've become—a piece of art."

"I guess," he said.

"Well, doesn't it make sense?"

He shrugged. He had never thought of it that way, even though he considered himself both a homebody and a thinker. Now it seemed obvious: a home—a piece of art.

After he got Jessica's lengthy poster-by-poster

review—a generic zoo, a sailboat crewed only by women, the Grand Canyon, and a koala cub in a tree—she asked him how the studio was going.

"Not great," he said.

"Why?"

"Oh, the vandalism's a pain, I'm getting phantom charges at Perry's, and Rita's started to bitch about my accounting system."

"I'm sorry you're having problems."

"It's just so much at one time."

"Don't they say problems always come in bunches or something?"

"I guess."

"Say, let's take that swim and forget all this depressing stuff."

Ramsay and Jessica took turns in the bathroom changing into their swimsuits, then took the elevator down to the pool.

"See what I was saying up there about the posters?" she said. "To show them to you is to show you who I am. It's one way for you to get to know me better."

"You like animals, women's rights, and wonders of the world."

"That's a start." She laughed. "But, for now, let's swim. Then you'll really get to know me! You go first."

Ramsay splashed into the dark wetness and treaded water. "The water's great," he said.

"Usually eighty, right on the button," she said.

"Come on in," he said. Their voices echoed through the pool area. Four orbs of soft light seemed to float in air, but each was mounted atop a six-foot tower.

"I used to swim competitively, you know," she said.

She stood there at poolside and slowly dropped her terry cover-up onto the deck. Now she wore only a red tank suit, almost transparent. Her nipples jutted into the poolside light, leaving sharp little shadows on her suit. A not-so-subtle mound of pubic hair glistened, too. Jessica propped herself for a racing dive, then smoothly cast her arms forward and sliced through the water at a nearly horizontal angle, barely making a sound.

She surfaced. "Mmm. It's wonderful."

"That was great. Where did you swim?" Ramsay asked. "College or something?"

"Actually, high school. Hyde Park, Illinois. The hundred-meter crawl and butterfly." She sipped a mouthful of water and shot a perfect arc.

"You're from Illinois, too?" he said. "Like Rita and Devlin."

"We ought to start a club," she said.

They chatted as they treaded water. Occasionally Jessica dipped her head backward. When she lifted her head, her hair lay down like satin. "So, why'd you get the divorce, Marcus?"

"Mainly because she wanted me to be someone I wasn't."

"Who was that?"

"Well, her dad was Mr. Corporate and she always saw me as a junior version of that." He spit water.

"So, what's wrong with that?" she asked.

"Nothing. Until I got fired."

"Oh, I see."

"I guess I wasn't the same in her eyes after that . . . hell, not even in my eyes. This photo thing was always just a lark to her."

"You sound really upset."

"The anger's still there. Not just at getting fired, but at her, too. I thought our relationship was more than the roles we played."

"It'll take time for you to heal."

"I guess." He hung his head.

"Say, can you do a surface dive?" she asked. She kicked her legs high, dived toward the bottom, then, a second later, resurfaced. The water streamed down her face.

He studied her. "Man, just now the line of your face looked like a cameo," he said.

"You're just saying that."

"No, honest," he said, "and you tread water like you've done it a lot."

"All those practices after school. My sister was always jealous of me," she said. "My swimming and my hands." Jessica gracefully waved her fingers in the air while she effortlessly treaded water.

"That's right. You said you were a twin. Suzette?"

"Suzanne. I told you; don't you remember? At the shoot."

"About two thirty-two in the afternoon?" he said, and laughed.

"You're mocking me," she said.

"No, I'm just teasing," he said. "Your memory is incredible."

"Suzanne and I are fraternal twins, but she looks a lot like me. I think I told you that. When we were kids, I was the tomboy; she was the dainty one."

"But you had the beautiful hands?"

"Hers aren't bad, either. She was the dancer back then, she could always float through the air—so gracefully."

"What's she doing now?"

"I told you."

"Park ranger, right?"

Jessica gurgled some water. "At Grand Canyon. I've always wanted to work down there. Just for grins, I send them my application every year. They write me a rejection, but they make it sound like I almost get in. You can tell they're just trying to cushion the blow."

"What does a ranger do?" he asked.

"Gives talks and leads hikes, especially to the canyon floor. Plus, Suzanne's a storyteller."

"A storyteller?"

"She can go on forever, reciting various Native American traditions and how we can learn from them. She's really something, the way she makes it a spiritual deal. She believes in the oneness of all things."

"Like the Buddhists?"

"Sort of."

"I like the sound of all that, but I've never learned how to incorporate that thinking into my life. I have trouble imagining it," he said.

"Suzanne would say you're missing out."

"I'll have to confer with her on that someday."

She gazed away for a second. "Right. Uh, let me see you swim. I can help you with your stroke."

"I think the crawl is my weakest." Ramsay splashed across the pool. He reached the other side and swam back.

"Not bad," she said, "but you need to use your legs more and lift your elbows uniformly out of the water, like an invisible string is pulling on them." She demonstrated, swimming perfectly across the pool and back.

"That was fantastic." He swam to the edge of the pool and back again, trying to mimic her. "How's that?" he asked.

"Better. But more like this. Come here." This time she stood close to him and moved his arms in the water. As she held them, she pushed her breasts into his elbows—he shuddered. It had been a long time since a woman had been that close, wearing so little. Her shoulder muscles glistened in the dark.

"What's the matter?" she asked. "You're shaking, Marcus. You having trouble with the deeper water?"

"I'm just not used to it." At that point, the way she held his wrists and commanded his every move through the water made him shiver.

Her eyes lingered as they met his. "I can tell you're nervous," she said, holding him close. As they both treaded water as one, she asked, "Why don't you kiss me, Marcus? I'm not going to bite your head off."

"Fine." He did, like he had been waiting for her permission and she had just given it. Her tongue met his. He pulled away, still treading water.

"That was really nice, so soft," Ramsay said. "It's hard to do this in the water."

"How's this?" she asked, then jumped at him and kissed him again, supporting him in the water with strong, thrusting whips of her legs. He closed his eyes and returned her kiss—it was wonderful.

Soon, their moans echoed through the pool area. As they thrashed about, Ramsay became concerned that they might be discovered by residents sitting next to open apartment windows situated around the pool's perimeter. Shaken from his spell, he pulled back. "Jessica, please stop." He gasped for air and held her back. "I don't think I can do this."

"Why not?"

"I'm sorry—it's the divorce."

"But wasn't that kiss perfect?" She panted. "I've needed that kind of intimacy for so-o-o long."

"I know it sounds dumb, but it feels like I'm cheating or something," he said.

"But, Marcus, your marriage is finished!"

"I know; I know. I'm as free as a bird. But I just don't feel like it yet. I still feel controlled by Kathy."

"I can see how the whole thing controls you."

He nodded and swore under his breath.

For a minute, neither Marcus nor Jessica said anything. The divorce talk had killed the romantic moment.

Jessica suddenly dunked him hard. As he opened his eyes, he saw a blurry nighttime world of water and flashes of light. When he surfaced, she dunked him again. He surfaced, gasping for breath, choking on water. "Why did you do that?" Ramsay asked. He grabbed the side of the pool.

"I've got to toughen you up so you can handle all the bullshit at the studio. Marcus, you have to see my sister. If I can't help you, I know she can." She smiled.

"Maybe. But really, it does look like things are beginning to turn around for me. Vanessa Franklin, that LA rep, wants to submit my shots to *Studio Photography* magazine. And I'm thinking of taking Tyler's advice—teaching my lighting technique."

"Cool."

"He thinks I should call the seminars *Ramsay on Light*. What do you think?"

"Sounds super."

"James Honeybear asked me to get more active in SIP, too."

"That group Stan Devlin started? I've been in some of his shots," she said. "He's good. At least, he acts like it."

"Actually, his style is sort of old-fashioned."

"Your shots don't even look like photographs."

"It's the way I apply the lighting."

"They're so cool."

"Listen, Jesse, I think I should go for tonight. My skin's all puckered," he said, "and I'm exhausted." Suddenly he pictured himself feeling perfectly content lying alone in bed.

"I thought you might stay for coffee," she said, "if we didn't go for pizza. What do you think?"

"Sorry, but I'd rather just go tonight," he said. "Maybe another time?"

"Shit," she said dejectedly. "Great date."

Suddenly he felt trapped by Jessica and needed to get away. "I'm sorry, Jessica. I had a good time, really."

Jessica grew agitated. "Oh, terrific." She splashed away, swimming to the far end of the pool. She climbed out, turned toward him, and spoke in an unembarrassed echo: "You know, Marcus, you really need to vent all this bullshit you've been through. You're a pain in the ass. Suzanne could do you some good."

He watched her storm into the building. She was right, he thought. It was time to conquer his losses. In retrospect, he knew he had been feeling wounded, sorry for himself.

Ramsay climbed out, toweled off, and walked inside. He took the elevator to the third floor and walked to her door. It was ajar and swung open when he touched it.

Jessica stood there, her eyes swollen and red. "Now what is it?" she asked.

"I'm sorry for being a jerk," he said. "You're right. I don't know whether I'm coming or going. I know I have to resolve my issues."

"Want some coffee now?" She sniffled. "I want you to know how much it means to me . . . to have you . . . you know, hang around with me. My doc says I've been alone too long. I need to form strong friendships."

"Sounds like a healthy idea."

She sniffled again. "It's true. Even though you tease me, you at least make me feel like I'm an okay person—part of your team and everything." She looked at the floor. "I admit that I like being with you."

"Well, thanks for that. Why don't we talk about me going down to see your sister? I can have a chat with her and see if she can help me with that healing stuff."

"Great; that sounds super."

He shrugged. "I figure, hocus-pocus or not, some healing might help me with a new start. What have I got to lose? The Native American stuff could be cool, too."

"I swear, you won't regret it," she said.

As Ramsay drove home, he thought about his life, which seemed complex all of a sudden. Now there was Jessica, who might become a closer friend, although he wasn't sure she was his type. Still, he wondered if love could blossom from this one tiny flirtatious evening.

As he drove home, scenarios involving Jessica and even Rita played in his head.

Ramsay thought of Kathy as he passed the Garden Grove freeway. Did he still love her? Had he ever? Or was his attraction to her born only of like interests and careers? For the first time he had a strong sense that his time with her was over and might have been ill-conceived.

Marcus felt somewhat close to Rita, but he was concerned about her motorcycle-and-drug past. He was apprehensive about her obsessed boyfriend. Marcus wondered what else could be lurking in the shadows of her past that could make a relationship with her—personal or business—more of a problem than an opportunity.

Then he pictured Suzanne, a Jessica look-alike who had a spiritual orientation. He wondered if she might appeal to him more than he ever expected.

The next day, the clique of SIP photographers met at Coco's restaurant to assess the progress of their plan.

"How's it going with Ramsay?" Stan Devlin asked the group: Art Zipper, Ken Potter, James Honeybear, and Steve Gerard.

"Well," Steve Gerard said, "he seems to be making some inroads. He just got the Conroy account. He shot Backman the other day and I heard he did great."

"I know. I'm pretty sure I lost them," Devlin said. "Man, that's thirty percent of my billings."

"Well, the insider approach isn't hurting yet," Art Zipper said in a macho tone, like he was reporting on his sector. "Ramsay just keeps repairing, replacing, and moving on, like his pockets are bottomless—damn MBA."

"We have to give it time to wear him down," Stan Devlin said. "We'll eventually make him want to pack up that Hosemaster of his and leave Orange County. Rita said he just got divorced, too, so now there's no reason for him to stay a day longer."

James Honeybear shook his head.

Art Zipper's eyes flared. "Stan, Perry says he's going down to study with Aaron Jones at his new place in Santa Fe. Maybe he'll even get better at that light painting stuff. He's stealing more of my smaller clients every day. Impressing them with that fancy lighting. Maybe we should get a little heavier with the guy."

"I think this undermining stuff is a bad idea," James Honeybear said. "It's like we're playing CIA games or something."

"But, Honeybear, it's not like we've done any rough stuff yet." Devlin shrugged. "And besides, Ramsay trusts you. So, don't go pimping out on us now."

"Well, what else can we do?" Honeybear asked.

"For one thing, we could get him to head up SIP. He wouldn't have time to steal any other accounts then. That might hurt him more than any of this prank stuff." Devlin laughed. "If that doesn't work, we can take other steps."

"Like what?" Zipper rubbed his hands together enthusiastically.

"We're not talking rough, right?" Potter asked. "We agreed, no rough stuff."

'Don't worry about it," Devlin said.

Honeybear shook his head. "This is nonsense."

"Well, come on," Zipper squealed. "Spill it, Stan."

Devlin leaned over to Zipper, put up the back of his hand, and whispered, "Tell you about it later."

8

Marcus Ramsay's apartment, Tustin

One month later Ramsay tossed the Caesar salad and felt shaky, like it was a first date. When the bell rang, his heart raced. He opened the door and there stood his ex-wife, Kathy Armstrong Ramsay.

They had agreed to check in with each other periodically after they split, just to see how things were going. This was the first time. Because they hadn't had any kids to perpetually bond them, they agreed that an occasional visit would be a good idea. The checking-in tradition would undoubtedly die over time as they met other people and started new lives. But, for now, they thought it might ease the difficulty of their divorce.

"You look nice," he said. She wore a flowing navy blue silk blouse, tight jeans, and worn boots left over from their Dallas days.

"Howdy," she said as she sauntered into the room. Her attitude made Marcus wonder if she was pretending to be unaffected by their reunion.

Both acted awkward at the omission of a hello kiss. Suddenly Marcus said, "Well . . . maybe we should."

"Yeah, it'd be okay," she said.

They ducked at each other like preening cranes, kissing each other quickly and pulling back.

"Hey, we shouldn't be afraid of one little kiss," he said.

"I suppose you're right."

He leaned over more purposefully and kissed her on the cheek. Then she returned the kiss, like a close cousin might have. After exchanging pleasantries, they stood by his two-by-five-foot bleached pine table.

"Where are your plates?" she asked.

"In there." He pointed to a cabinet.

"You do the pasta; I do the sauce?" she asked.

"Like the old days."

Marcus went to the stove. He tipped the pasta into a colander to drain the water while she retrieved the bubbling marinara sauce from the microwave.

The salad was good, the pasta al dente, the sauce tangy, the wine Rutherford Hill merlot.

"Good wine," he said. "Remember?"

"Yes."

'To you," he said, "and your promotion at Pepe's."

"You know, I'm the first."

"First what?"

"First woman VP over there."

"Well, then let's toast again," he said. "You broke through the glass ceiling."

"And to you," she said. "Your success with the business. I admit the VP stuff feels sort of empty because I'm not sharing it with somebody."

"Really?" he said.

"It's true."

They smiled at each other. "So, I was worth something, then?" he asked.

"Yeah."

"I just got back from a trip," Ramsay said.

"Oh? Where?" she asked.

"Studying with my mentor—the guy who started light painting, Aaron Jones. He moved from San Francisco to Santa Fe."

"A seminar?"

"Yeah. His wife stuck by him, and now his light painting product, that Hosemaster, is a big success nationally."

She hung her head. Ramsay was sure she had taken his words as a not-so-subtle attack. He hadn't followed the Armstrong lifelong plan: "Stay with a company till you retire or die"—something her dad had recommended one Thanksgiving.

"You know, I shouldn't have been surprised at your success in the Abyss," Ramsay said. "It was in your blood."

"Still calling it that?" she asked.

"Well, it's the institution that destroyed my career and my marriage. Do you blame me for being cynical about it?"

"I . . . guess not," she said.

"Since there are so many photographers out there, I'm going to be hosting my own lighting seminars—Tyler's idea. He's my assistant."

"Sounds impressive." Her eyebrows rose.

"We'll pull shooters from San Diego to LA. I'll call the seminars *Ramsay on Light*."

"Sounds like a fast climb in your new profession."

"You can achieve something without the aid of an institution."

"I guess."

He sipped on his wine. "And the SIP guys want me to join the board. Maybe even be president."

"That's really cool."

"I think they respect the diversity I've brought to the photo community here," he said. "MBA, light painting, and all. Being president's special around Orange County since it's such a tight-knit community. Being the leader of one of the art organizations is pretty special."

"No kidding," she said.

"So, I guess I didn't do the photo thing on a whim, then?"

"I admit I am a little surprised." Her eyes flashed.

After dinner, the plates were stowed in the dishwasher and they retired to the puffy leather couch Ramsay had bought for himself after their split.

"Nice couch," she said.

"Great for necking."

They laughed.

"Kathy, I'm really proud of you," Marcus said to her in a soft voice. "Really, kudos to you."

"Hey, back to you, Marcus," Kathy said. "I couldn't have pulled off running on my own like that—and progressing so fast."

"It does feel good."

"It's nice to see you successful." She smiled. "After Texas, I never thought I'd see you happy."

"In spite of the garbage I've had to put up with."

"What garbage?"

"Oh, a bunch of weird stuff—it's nothing really."

"You think you're over Texas yet? Maybe you're super-achieving to make up for that bad stuff."

"Could be. I'm still carrying a lot of anger. It's buried deep. I was a star at that damn company, you know? Then I got fired because Hickman was so afraid." Ramsay sighed deeply. "I'm not over how unfair it was. And I really did feel possessed by James Post's spirit to make things right for him."

She chuckled. "It still sounds a little weird to me."

"I really did learn a lot from that experience."

She cuddled closer. "I think it's a major epiphany that you can talk about it so freely," she said.

"Time heals, I guess," he said and smiled. "I might even be ready to try some of those Native American healing ceremonies I told you about."

"That spiritual stuff sounds like you. Sometimes I think that's all that's ever motivated you."

"She leaned over and whispered, "What they did to you just wasn't fair."

"I thought I'd work for them forever." He hung his head.

"It's over now," she said. "I hope your new success will last."

"Really?" he said. "Remember? This is how we used to watch TV," he said.

She snuggled into him.

"Do you want me to kiss you, honey?" he asked and moved close.

She stared into space, then stood up suddenly. "Wait, Marcus. I think I'd better be the one who ends this," she said, "because I know you can't." She grabbed her coat and left without looking back.

"No other nominations?" Art Zipper asked as he scrawled Stan Devlin's name on the blackboard at the next SIP meeting. "Just Stan?"

Stan Devlin stood in front of the attendees and folded his arms across his chest. He smirked like a court jester who had just performed a feat impossible for contenders to match.

As a hush formed, Chester Major raised his hand and said, "I nominate Marcus Ramsay."

Devlin shot a squinted gaze at Ramsay.

"Well, Ramsay. Do you accept?" Zipper grunted.

"I guess, okay," Ramsay replied as the crowd murmured.

"Any seconds?" Zipper asked.

A half-dozen hands rose.

Zipper looked at Devlin for his approval—Devlin nodded.

Zipper scribbled Ramsay's name on the board.

"No others?" Zipper asked. "Fine. Everybody write down your votes and pass them up."

After the meeting's refreshment break, the members returned to their seats. Zipper stood and walked hesitantly to the front with a piece of paper in his hand. He copied the names on the board:

Marcus Ramsay	President
James Honeybear	Vice President
Elise Barker	Treasurer
Margaret Corbett	Secretary
Don Weiner	Member-at-Large
Stan Devlin	Member-at-Large

After the meeting, the newly elected officers convened at the Red Lion Inn in Costa Mesa, a singles' hot spot, for a postelection celebration.

"So, Ramsay's president." Zipper grinned.

"Congratulations, Marcus," Stan Devlin said. "I hope your term will be successful." He reached across the table to shake hands with Marcus.

"Thanks, Stan," Ramsay replied.

"You'll have lots of work ahead of you." He smiled. "You'll need to improve the newsletter, have a membership drive, and create a photographic assistant's source list."

"Well, my computer'll help," Ramsay said.

"Sure. Uh-huh."

As Ramsay sat there with the group of guys—the almighty clique he had observed from a distance just weeks before—he wondered about being the president of the organization. Would they expect him to play out their expectations of commercial photography's future in Orange County? Or could he strike out in new directions that they might not have considered or desired?

"It's gonna be a real challenge," Ramsay said.

Many eyes glanced Stan Devlin's way.

Ramsay watched the response curiously. He wondered why they looked at one another so approvingly, as if his elevation might have been preordained.

"I hope I can do the office justice," Ramsay said as he looked at his watch. "Say, I really gotta get going." He stood. "Got a shoot first thing tomorrow."

Stan Devlin smiled as he considered how Marcus had just successfully wooed the photographic body politic with his smooth-talking, educated crap. Now that Ramsay would be so busy, he would have difficulty dealing with the dirty tricks designed to undermine his studio's operation.

In fact, by shocking Marcus with a myriad of future

obstacles, Devlin could render the MBA competitor helpless. As he considered the bigger surprises he had planned, power flushed through Devlin. His position as chief warlord of all Orange County photographers never should've been in doubt.

Ramsay drove home from the SIP installation meeting. His election as the group's president had been virtually unanimous. Stan Devlin, as gracious as ever, had said a few words to bless the installation. It had been simple and uneventful, as if it had been planned.

Now the work would start, Ramsay thought as he drove into the dark. Tomorrow, besides his shoot, he would begin designing a new SIP newsletter. Also, he might be able to bolster attendance by improving the monthly meetings and initiating a sorely needed membership drive.

He knew it wouldn't be difficult to put his mark on the fumbling organization, but he was concerned about the time commitment.

He sped down Newport Avenue toward his apartment thinking of his date with Kathy. He had felt close to her like in the old days—for a little while. Then he remembered her hasty exit.

The possibility of returning to her raced through his head but departed just as fast. He realized that he'd never be accepted by her or her parents.

He also thought of his midnight swim with Jessica. It was nice to have a woman lust after you because of who you were, how you talked, and how you looked. And she obviously appreciated his interest in her. He wondered how he might react to her sister, the park ranger.

Thinking of the possibility of something going right

with a woman filled Ramsay with optimism. Maybe someone special was out there after all, waiting to brighten his future.

He thought of conducting his own *Ramsay on Light* seminars, too. Could he really lay claim to expert status after spending only a short time at his new studio, practicing in Texas, and studying with Aaron Jones? Would anyone come to his seminars?

On his way home, Ramsay stopped at the studio to review the books and see how the business was doing. He opened the car door, got out, and looked across the dark lot. Having his name on the door meant so much more that he had been picked as the president of the local photography organization.

I guess I've really made it, he thought.

On his way to the front door, he stopped. He looked up at the soffit over his suite's entry. It was not normal for it to be totally dark. The security light, which automatically came on at sunset, had burnt out. He felt his way along the door and put the key in. He went inside and locked the door behind him.

Sitting at his desk with only his office light burning, Marcus started up his Macintosh. In a few seconds, the *Maccountant* screen flashed. He opened the file "Photo 86"—his books. He skipped past the "Revenue" account to "Accounts Receivable."

"Weird," he said.

He compared his cash balance with the register of "Accounts Receivable Paid-Off." He was thinking there shouldn't be much of a difference because he hadn't made any major purchases.

But there was—almost ten thousand dollars not in his

favor! He searched the deposit book for evidence that several large checks had been cashed, which would explain the discrepancy, but he found a problem. Several large checks, totaling ninety-six hundred dollars, had been cashed but never deposited into his account.

He gulped.

This was the side of the business he had entrusted to Rita Scorpino. Since he had hired the formal legal firm controller from Elk Grove Village, Illinois, he had become satisfied that she was capably running the financial side of things.

Now he wasn't so sure.

But still, he tried another tactic. He called up all accounts receivable for the same period. Again, they didn't match—a difference of just under ten thousand dollars.

It didn't make any sense. He'd have to wait to ask Rita about it until Friday, when she was due to return from Palm Springs. It was the day before his first *Ramsay on Light* seminar.

Would she really steal from me? he wondered.

It was incomprehensible.

Suddenly Marcus had the feeling that things weren't going as smoothly as he had surmised. He felt panicky. But, if Rita had stolen from him, the computer records would be all the evidence he'd need to prosecute her—he frantically printed out key account information and copied pages of his deposit book.

Only minutes before, he had felt so high, having been elected president by his peers and thinking about holding his own lighting seminars. But now he shifted into a defensive mode, feeling like he could trust no one, not even Rita. Like the night he was fired, his stomach clenched with stage fright–type pangs. The sober cynic had returned.

Later, as he armed the studio's burglar alarm and slipped out the front door, he looked around the parking lot and beyond, to the field across Parkway Loop. He wondered how he could have mistakenly pegged Rita as honest, sweet, and friendly. Was the little-girl voice, the dry sense of humor, and the gregarious demeanor she displayed with clients *not* who she was? Had he failed to recognize a Henry Hyde side of her?

He climbed in his Jeep and swerved out of the lot. "I should've seen this coming. I'm such a fool," he muttered. *Nobody is as nice as they seem—not even Rita.*

A possibility flashed by him, one he hadn't considered until now. Her past experience with heavy drugs, her trouble with the police, her being fired from the law firm, her baby-like dependence on her parents, and her obsessed boyfriend, Harvey, had never made sense before. Now the disparate parts were fitting together.

9

Marcus Ramsay Photographic

The next day Ramsay's assignment was shooting a trombone on a painted muslin backdrop for an Orange County Performing Arts Center brochure. It seemed a simple enough shot. But to uniformly light the bell of the tarnished trombone, he would have to create a light tent of tracing paper around the top of the instrument, supported by stands that would be invisible in the reflection of the horn. He planned to shine several lights through the tracing paper to uniformly light the bell. By reflecting the light tent, the old trombone would look brand-new and tarnish-free.

In thirty minutes Tyler and Marcus had built the light tent. The tarnished trombone, lying on the painted backdrop, instantly looked brand-new. But now there were no shadows falling on the backdrop—the trombone looked like it was in limbo.

"What do we do now?" Tyler said, perplexed. "That looks weird."

"Pretty tough."

"You looked bugged today, Marcus."

"It's nothing."

"Just a bad day?" Tyler pushed.

'No. I'm bugged all right . . . ten grand worth."

Tyler crunched his forehead. "Ten . . . grand?"

"I think Rita's been stealing from me."

"You're kidding!"

"Don't say anything, okay?"

"By the way, where is she today?"

"She asked for a few days off to visit a friend in Palm Springs. Last night I was toying with the books and discovered she was probably ripping me off."

"How can you be sure?"

"The books don't lie. It looks like she embezzled ten grand."

"How?"

"She cashed some checks and kept the money. Then she recorded them as deposited."

"Jeez."

"Tyler?"

"Yeah?"

"I think I was wrong about you. Rita implied that you might have stolen some equipment. Meanwhile, she's been the culprit all along. I should've seen it."

"You thought I was stealing?"

"Well, I want you to know I'm sorry for suspecting you."

"Thanks . . . I guess."

"God, I feel so paranoid. I just don't know who to trust." Ramsay slammed the work table.

"Marcus?" Tyler said.

"Yeah?"

Tyler put his arm on Marcus's shoulder. "You can trust me, really."

Ramsay sighed deeply. "Thanks."

"Say, let's work on the positive. Your lighting seminars are gonna be a smash, right?"

Ramsay smiled. "I hope so. I could use some good news."

For several hours they studied their shadowless trombone shot like two guys standing around a car in disrepair: if they scratched their chins long enough, the answer would magically appear.

Solving the problem wasn't going to be easy. By dismantling the light tent, they could add beautiful shadows. Keeping the light tent would eliminate the shadows, but create the illusion that the trombone was floating.

Ramsay had a thought. "Tyler, go get me some gray-colored pencils."

Minutes later, Tyler returned with several colored pencils: cool gray, warm gray, and others that were neither cool nor warm.

With his Hosemaster fiber-optic lighting device, Ramsay created a shadow of the trombone on the backdrop. For a while, he just stared at the shadow. He compared it to each of the colored pencils—the shadow's color was similar to the bluish-gray pencil. He put the others aside.

Leaving the light tent in place, Ramsay proceeded to draw a thin shadow around the edge of the trombone, directly on the muslin. At first it looked like drawn-on colored pencil, but after he rendered the pencil more uniformly, it took on the homogeneity of a real shadow.

"This might work," Ramsay said. "Call it a manufactured shadow."

"Cool." Tyler fired the strobe lights.

"Sometimes you can have your cake and eat it, too," Ramsay said.

Minutes later, the final flashes perfectly lit the trombone's bell and the hand-drawn "shadow" made the instrument look solidly positioned on the painted muslin.

"That's such a cool trick. You should include it in your seminar," Tyler said.

"That reminds me; we have to get ready."

The phone rang.

Marcus went to the phone and picked it up. "Marcus Ramsay Photographic?"

"Dearie!"

"Vanessa." It was Vanessa Franklin, the artist's rep from LA.

"I've got great news," she said. "*Studio Photography* magazine wants to feature you in their September issue."

"You're kidding."

"Really! Seven pages. Can you believe it? I sent them your promo pieces. Listen to this. They want to call it 'Ramsay's Light.' What do you think?" she asked.

"Great title—my fifteen minutes of fame! Thanks for believing in me, Vanessa."

"Now you have to let me represent you. I've already got a contract prepared, and I never do that. What do you think?"

"I'm so glad Donald got us together," he said.

"He's a great fellow, eh?" she said.

For the rest of the afternoon Marcus and Tyler practiced various lighting experiments for the *Ramsay on Light* seminar.

In his excitement, Ramsay forgot he'd be talking to Rita the next day.

Saturday at the studio, a group of fifteen photographers—some amateurs, some pros—sat on the edges of their folding chairs. Tyler and Rita, assistants for the seminar, scurried about.

Marcus adjusted his mike. "Test, test. Welcome to the first *Ramsay on Light*." Ramsay watched as Rita set up the first lighting demonstration. He felt agitated about confronting her later.

Once they were under way, the small transmitter microphone projected Ramsay's voice uniformly around the studio. Each slide loomed large on the sixteen-foot-high studio wall.

"To apply light is all about *seeing*," he said. "Without light, there is nothing. Light only shows itself as it reflects off a subject. Otherwise, it is only invisible energy."

The students leaned forward.

He set up a small cardboard poster. "Photography utilizes a negative palette." He pointed to a diagram on the poster. "See, it starts with one hundred percent black. Then, as the pallette, or film emulsion, is used up, there remains less and less of it to *record* additional light."

The students looked a bit confused. "This is the first time I've heard it explained like this," one of them said. "At school, darkroom chemicals and photographic paper were all that was important. Here we're talking about light, not just the effects of it."

"In actual fact, *photo-graph* means 'light-write,'" Ramsay said. "If you look at your subject casually, you will only simulate the concept of the subject that you've been carrying around for a lifetime. To see the light, you must look closely at the way it interacts with the subject—every shadow and highlight. It's a matter of focusing attentiveness."

Afterward Ramsay sat in his office, reading his evaluation forms. Tyler appeared at his door. "It was great, but different than I expected," Tyler said. "Now I understand that I don't need fancy diagrams to show me where to put the lights. I just have to see the light."

"Exactly."

Ramsay wanted to share his seminar's success with someone else. Still at his desk, he picked up the phone. He heard Stan Devlin's voice on the line scolding Rita. Ramsay hung up. He took a deep breath, got up, and walked to the reception desk.

As Ramsay saw Rita slam the phone down, he was filled with dread. "Why did Stan want to talk to you?" Ramsay asked. "Why did he sound so unhappy?"

"Uh, because I didn't tell him my brother was coming out here later this summer." Rita crunched her brow defensively, wary, like a little kid about to cry.

"Rita, we have to talk."

"I need Monday off," Rita said. She rose abruptly.

"But," Ramsay said, "you just had the last few days off."

She stood, looking panicky.

"Rita? What is it?"

"Just . . . see you Tuesday," she said, and started to run out the door, not looking back.

"Wait, Rita!" Ramsay called. Now he'd have to wait to discuss the embezzled money. *I might not ever see her again,* he thought as he watched her swerve out of the lot.

A fifty-year-old woman, one of Ramsay's students, appeared at the door to the reception area. "Excuse me, but is there a problem?" she asked.

"No. Just typical studio stuff. You're Sylvia, right?"

"D'Angelas."

"Can I help you?" he asked.

"Well, I have a question."

"What is it?"

"Recently I was bumped from a sharing situation at a studio in Santa Ana. So, I'm looking for a new space, but maybe we should talk another time."

"I do have this office up front," he said.

"I shoot mostly weddings, so there wouldn't be any conflict between us."

"Sounds good. We can talk about it. Right now I'm just dealing with a bunch of garbage."

"Garbage?"

"You don't want to hear about it."

"Something about that assistant, the lady who went running out? Rita, right?"

"Yeah. Sorry to say, I caught her with her hand in the till."

"My Lord! A lot?"

"A lot. I'm deciding how I need to handle this." Full of emotion spawned from his day, Ramsay half-cried and half-talked. "Sorry to burden you with this. I've been dealing with a divorce and losing my last job. But you probably don't want to hear—"

"You had another job?" She gestured around the studio with the question.

"The studio came after I left a corporate job. The studio was supposed to be my new start. Right in the middle of the start-up, my wife dumped me."

"I don't blame you for being angry," she said.

"Thanks, but I really don't need to bore you with all this."

"I bet you feel wounded, too, huh?" She nodded her head knowingly.

He nodded.

"Jerry's been through the corporate thing. He's my husband. Took him years to recover."

"Years? Jeez."

"Now he's better."

"What finally did it?" he asked.

"He finally realized it was okay to be vulnerable . . . and he mourned."

"Cried?" Ramsay asked.

"Mourned. For a week—no, it was a month. He cried a lot and talked about it constantly. He allowed himself to grieve over what could have been, admit his loss, and accept his vulnerability. The stronger you think you are in your job, the harder you fall if you're fired."

"That explains how I feel."

"You probably haven't let your guard down, right?" she asked. "Still trying hard to make it work?"

"That's me." He laughed. "I keep myself busy running a business, leading an organization, and doing this seminar."

"I'm so sorry," she said.

He looked at her. Concern radiated from her eyes.

On Monday, after Ramsay talked on the phone to the assistant district attorney about Rita, Sylvia, who had started renting the front office for $350 a month, chattered away as she made phone calls to leads for her wedding business.

Ramsay made a call to follow-up on a bid he had sent to a potential client. He asked the art director whom he would be bidding against. When the man said Stan Devlin, Ramsay felt sure he would get an affirmative call later. Devlin probably bid the number he had advocated so fervently at the SIP meetings, fifteen hundred dollars a day.

After lunch, a return call came. But the substance of it was a surprise.

"I'm sorry . . ." the art director said. "Another photographer got the assignment."

"May I ask who?"

The art director told him.

"Stan Devlin?" Ramsay asked.

"Yes. His bid was lower," the art director said.

"Couldn't be. I bid one thousand."

"He bid eight hundred."

"Eight? My impression was that he never made a bid less than fifteen."

"That's where you both started, but he came down twice. Then we settled at eight."

"You're sure? Stan Devlin?" Ramsay asked.

"Yeah. Devlin always gets our business. He prices more aggressively than the rest of you guys."

"It surprises me that he bid so low."

"Well, maybe next time."

Ramsay hung up. He realized that Devlin had indeed been treating his business like an oil cartel: Out of one side of his mouth, he chided his compatriots into bidding fifteen-hundred a day, like it was religion; out of the other side, he bid much less to ensure he would win the assignments. Ramsay figured Devlin had probably been doing it for years.

Marcus walked up to the front office to recount his story to Sylvia. She softly lectured him about the value of allowing himself to be vulnerable and how that would diffuse his anger. She explained how he could replace his negative thoughts with positive energy.

"Sorry. I'm not into that energy stuff," Marcus said, impatient with her jibberish. "But, say, can you lock up tonight?" Still flustered about Devlin, he left.

"At some point it'll make sense," Sylvia called to him as the door shut.

10

Society of Illustrative Photographers' meeting, Steve Gerard's studio, Costa Mesa, California

The next SIP monthly meeting was at Steve Gerard's studio. It was Ramsay's first as president. The group of photographers—accustomed to Stan Devlin's preaching—fidgeted as Marcus Ramsay stood at the podium. But they began to relax as he promised stimulating programs, interesting speakers, and regular elections.

"SIP will exist more for its members. You won't hear a word on pricing." He looked at Stan Devlin. "I promise you."

They all applauded, except Devlin.

Later, as Ramsay walked through the crowd, he approached Stan, who was downing a can of beer. "Stan?" Ramsay asked.

"What?"

"I talked to one of your clients the other day. You dramatically underbid me . . . and won."

"What?" Devlin asked, surprised.

"You heard me."

"I don't know what you're talking about," he said, fidgeting with his can.

"I figured out what you've been doing all these years. You've encouraged all the other shooters to bid high; then you underbid and get the business—nice ploy."

Devlin sneered. "Shut up, you know-it-all MBA." He turned around and huffed out of Gerard's studio.

Chester Major walked up to Ramsay. "He's just pissed because you're the new president."

"At the least," Ramsay said.

"He's a union dickhead if you ask me," Major said.

"The meeting was great," Ramsay said to Jessica on the phone the next day. "So was the *Ramsay on Light*."

"You sound happy," she said. "That's a nice change."

"It is. How are things with the modeling and acting?" he asked.

"The new promo cards with your pictures went out, so I'll see if they help. And, my acting classes are stupendous: The teacher thinks I'm a natural. Maybe I'm not as pretty as some of 'em, but he says it's good that I tend to the detail in my roles, like Meryl Streep."

"How's your sister?" he said. "Suzanne, right?"

"Yeah. I wish I could do what she does at the canyon. She buys into the oneness of all things. She's so spiritual. They love her down there."

"Does she have your edge?"

"What do you mean?" she asked.

"Well, you can get a little snappy sometimes, I'd say. A little brittle."

"Brittle?" she said.

"Well, a little," he said.

"Do you have to judge me, Marcus?" she asked. "You're always doing that."

"Listen, I'm really sorry."

"It's just that sometimes you judge others like you think you're better than them. You're sure not acting like you want to swim with me again," she said.

"But I do," Ramsay said.

"Are you just saying that? I thought only I liked it last time."

"Why are you being so paranoid?"

"Now you're saying I'm paranoid," she said. "Can't you say anything nice?"

He rolled his fingers.

"What's wrong now?" she asked. "You're being so quiet."

"Nothing. Listen; I'm gonna say good-bye. I'm tired of you trying to trip me up in my own words."

"You're pissed."

"Yes, I am," he said. "This bickering is annoying."

"You mean I'm annoying,"

"Jesse, can't we stop the bickering?"

"You called me Jesse."

"So?"

"Suzanne always called me that."

Ramsay crunched his brow. "Called?"

"She used to," she said.

Ramsay got to work early on Tuesday to make sure he'd arrive before Rita. Over the weekend he had rehearsed how he would confront her.

He heard reveille sound at the marine base as he sat at his desk, shaking from stress. In less than an hour, he would accuse Rita *and* fire her at the same time.

At ten after eight, Rita came laughing through the front door of the studio. She had obviously heard something funny on the radio and carried it in with her, mumbling the joke over and over. She walked into Ramsay's office with a chuckle. When she saw him standing behind his desk, her smile disappeared.

"We have to talk, Rita," Ramsay said. He swallowed, then cleared his throat and he fiddled with his heavy pen.

Rita shuffled uneasily in place, adjusting her belt, then her earrings. "What's up?"

Ramsay didn't laugh.

"What's going on?" she asked.

"We need to talk about the money."

She turned ashen.

"Rita, I know you stole it," he said.

"You can't prove anything," she said.

"I have proof and I've already talked to the DA—you're in trouble."

She suddenly sucked in air. "Fuck you!" She turned and stomped out of his office.

"Rita, it's over," he called and walked after her.

"Just try!" She kept walking through the client area.

"I'll get all of it back. I swear!" Ramsay yelled.

She rushed through the reception area.

"You can't run from this, Rita," he said and bounded after her.

As Rita huffed out of the studio, Ramsay followed her to the front door.

She ran across the parking lot mumbling, "Asshole."

Ramsay stood there and watched her get into her car and frantically drive away. Rita, his fellow innocent Midwesterner, was no longer innocent. Now she would be a marked felon.

That afternoon, Marla Sanderson, the assistant DA, called Ramsay. A bench warrant for Rita's arrest would be issued the next day. He gave her Rita's address.

Three months later, the court calendar freed up. Ramsay was notified that he would be testifying the following week. He sat at his desk and pondered what his testimony would be.

Just then, the phone rang. It was Jessica. "Well, Marcus, you up for another swim?"

"I'm free this Friday night," Ramsay said.

"I'll call you Thursday to confirm," she asked.

"I guess," he said.

"You guess?"

"Fine. But I do have my seminar on Saturday. I'll need my beauty sleep," he said.

"You can come over at eight. We'll swim, then eat. It won't be late. I promise."

Ramsay drove north to LA on Friday evening. *Jessica Dasher was a brilliant woman*, he thought, as he reviewed the short time he'd known her. She was quirky, yes, but she also displayed incredible insights. While her banter was merciless, it was mixed with comments that occasionally bordered on idolatry. The banter annoyed him, but when she flooded his ego with praise he felt truly appreciated.

Sometimes she seemed to drift away to another world. "If you were only mine, Marcus," she'd say sadly, "I mean all mine . . . ," she'd sigh. "Sometimes I am so-o-o lonely." Then she would add some indistinct love vow. "You'd probably just hate me," she'd say. "You're always preoccupied with your losses. We'll have to take care of them." And then she'd mention Suzanne.

Jessica frequently sounded like she was punishing herself. Each chattery conversation with Ramsay started with some form of negative self-debasement: the nattiness of her hair, the tackiness of her car, or the inadequacy of her breasts.

In response, Ramsay found himself bolstering her up—he wondered if she intended that dynamic all along. At the end of their conversations, her eyes glowed with feelings of pure love. Ramsay was so confused!

Now, as he approached LA, he was guessing that talking was the only kind of intercourse they'd have this time. He would refuse the physical act until he knew it was born of true love, from both his side and hers.

Twenty minutes later they climbed out of the pool after a brief dip. The sensual touching so prevalent in the first swim had been replaced by bland chitchat.

"Boy, that was passionate," she said sarcastically.

"I just wanted to see you again, Jessica. And talk—that's all."

They walked up the stairs to her apartment. "I'm sorry," he said. "I've had Rita's case on my mind. I talked to the assistant DA again today. I go to court next week. And I have my seminar tomorrow. I'm under a lot of pressure right now."

Jessica opened the door to her apartment. They went in.

"That's it?" Jessica said as she turned to him. "But are you saying you don't like my body?"

"Jessica, I don't feel like contemplating your breasts tonight. I just have this case on my mind."

She sighed audibly. "Okay . . . what about it?"

"They say I definitely have a case."

"Was there any doubt?" she asked.

"I wasn't so sure. They issued the bench warrant a

long time ago, but yesterday I found out there's an opening on the court calendar next week."

"That's great. Lock the bitch up," Jessica said.

"Oh yeah—the DA is going to talk to Rita's lawyer about a plea bargain. If she pleads guilty to grand larceny, the embezzlement charges will get dropped. She'll go to jail for five to seven years."

"Is that good?"

"I guess. If she insists on a jury, she'll risk serving ten to twelve. If her lawyer's any good, she won't try that."

"What about the money? Ten grand's a lot."

"They recovered three when they searched Rita's folks' place in Huntington," Ramsay said.

"Search warrant? I bet they loved that."

"Really. I'm guessing she went to Vegas the day she said she was heading to Palm Springs. She probably gambled the other seven grand away." He shook his head. "Rita'll be paying me forever when she gets out of prison."

"They do installments?"

"Maybe a hundred or two a month. She can't miss a payment—it's a condition of parole."

"Can you imagine being locked up for seven years?"

They toweled off and alternated getting dressed in her bathroom.

A few minutes later Jessica and Marcus got in her Geo Metro. Jessica drove to the California Pizza Kitchen on Ventura Boulevard.

Once in CPK, they waited for their table. Then they were seated.

"Hmm." In front of him, she shed her T-shirt, leaving only a skimpy, damp tank top that displayed the strength in her shoulders and, simultaneously, her chest and erect nipples. As she stretched like a cat, shaking her wet hair, her eyes glimmered at him as if she were giving him a private striptease.

"You like what you see, don't you, Marcus?" she asked. "This is what appeals to you, right?"

"I guess." He shrugged.

"My top?" She cocked her head and looked down at her chest. She tweaked her nipples.

Ramsay was surprised at the way she displayed herself. It was so garish and obvious. "Sure, I like it...I guess."

"Boy, that's convincing," she said. "What can I do to impress you? Be a ranger down at the park like my sister, Suzanne?"

Jessica closed her eyes and rocked side-to-side in a trance, her arms dangling at her sides.

"Excuse me, but can I break in?" Ramsay asked. "Does Suzanne look like you, Jessica? Exactly?"

"I'm a few pounds lighter." She closed her eyes and kept rocking.

"When can I meet her and talk about this healing stuff?" he asked. "I think I'm ready now."

She stopped rocking suddenly, opened her eyes, and glared at him. "Really?"

"I was thinking about that trip to the canyon soon. Could I see her then?"

Jessica paused, cleared her throat, and said, "Hmm."

"What do you think?"

"I happen to know she's taking a few days off soon," she said.

"Do you want to go with me to see her?"

"Sorry. I have a busy schedule the next two months. The agency is sending me to Dallas, Denver, and the Bay Area."

"Too bad. I'll have to bring her your best wishes, then."

Jessica paused in thought for a second. "You sure could use a spiritual kick in the ass, though. It would jump-start you back to normal. Even though I can't go with, we're always together, she and I—you know, the twin thing." Her eyes drooped sadly at their edges.

"You okay?" He looked at his watch. "Say, Jessica. You can't keep me out too late the night before my seminar," Ramsay said. "I do need to get my sleep, and it's a long drive home."

"Let's order then." She raised a water glass toward the waiter. "We should celebrate your second *Ramsay on Light*. So, the idea's catching on?"

"Yeah. Got a full house this time. Hope it goes as well as the first one."

"Well, there's no reason it shouldn't, right?" she said.

The next day, Saturday, in the steel gray of dawn, Ramsay pulled into the business park. He was meeting Tyler early to set up the chairs and prep the sweet rolls and coffee. The rest of the production—lighting demonstrations, charts, and sound system—had been fine-tuned during the final two days of rehearsal and was ready to go.

He pulled up to the front of his suite.

What? White smoke was rising from the rear of his building.

He drove around back and couldn't believe his eyes. A fire truck rumbled immediately behind his suite. Its hose was strewn across the parking lot to a hydrant amid rising smoke and puddles of water. A handful of firemen rustled about, apparently cleaning up.

Ramsay pulled up and jumped out of his Jeep. "What the hell is going on?" he asked the lead fireman.

"Who are you?" The man looked up from busily filling out a form on his clipboard.

The back of Ramsay's suite was blown open. The ten-foot garage door hung from its roller—a rippled hunk of metal. Chalky masonry chunks and drywall bits littered the parking lot for fifty feet in a near-perfect semicircle around the door.

"I'm the owner, Marcus Ramsay," he said as he squinted through the smoke and steam. "What happened?"

"Explosion, Mr. Ramsay," he said. "Plenty big. They called you ten minutes ago, but you just left your place, because we got your machine. We were here in seconds, so the fire only hurt a little. The explosion did all the damage. You have any chemicals in there?"

"Some paint thinner is all. We don't have a darkroom." Ramsay was stunned. "My seminar's impossible now."

"Seminar?"

"I had a photo seminar scheduled for today."

"Sorry, sir. Somebody did your place real good. They took out that tool shop, and those kitchen walls are half-gone. The rest is just space, right?"

"Yeah."

The fireman shook his head. "Never seen one quite so bad."

"What about the offices up front?" Ramsay asked.

"Not even touched. You got any enemies out there? Somebody have a grudge?"

"Not that I know of."

"That's the first thing the arson boys'll ask, you know. This was no accident; I can tell. Nothing to even suggest an accident. This was planned."

The rear of the building was decimated. The wall that Ramsay had built to separate the tool shop from the main shooting area was a crumpled mess. The steel studs lay there like a twisted Erector Set.

"Who would do this?" Ramsay kicked at the rubble. Strobes, power packs, and light stands had been pulled from the rubble and put into a pile. All except two of them were twisted and melted, dripping with water.

Just then Tyler ran up. "What happened?" he asked.

Ramsay mumbled, "Maybe this is a sign I should close the studio."

"No kidding," Gonzales said drearily, looking around, shaking his head. "This is unbelievable."

"Business been bad?" the fireman asked, poised to take more notes.

"Not the best, but getting better."

"Well, this explosion was an expert job for sure," the fireman said. "If they wanted to, they could've blown the whole place up; I can tell you that."

"Is that possible?" Ramsay said.

"Oh, yeah," he said.

"Must've been those vandals from Santa Ana," Ramsay said. "You know, when I was first starting up they stole a microwave out of the back of the studio in broad daylight. We just turned our heads for a second—gone."

"Could be the gangs, all right," the fireman said. "It's obvious they knew how to hit you just where it would hurt. Mr. Ramsay, you got insurance, right?"

"Yeah, the best, why?" Ramsay asked.

"Just wondering."

"Maybe it was the clique." Tyler Gonzales shrugged. "They hate you, I bet."

Ramsay thought back to how the clique objected to his anti-price-fixing notions. "Naw, they might hate my ideas, but they wouldn't do this. This is criminal."

"Want my opinion?" a gritty fireman asked as he walked up.

"What?"

"The explosion was big enough to cash in good."

"You're not accusing me, are you?" Ramsay looked exasperated.

"I'm just saying somebody wanted to cash in good."

"I resent that implication," Ramsay said.

"Hey, Jenkins," the head fireman said, "now's not the time to go pointing fingers."

"I was just speculating," Jenkins said.

Minutes later the first of Ramsay's students arrived. He mumbled and kicked around the explosion site. "We get our money back, right?" he asked Ramsay.

"Yes," Ramsay said.

Later that night an old black-and-white episode of *Perry Mason* played on TV. Marcus Ramsay sat in his easy chair, staring as he slowly sipped his merlot and stroked his wineglass.

The next Tuesday, Ramsay was called into court to testify against Rita. It was the first time in ages he had worn a suit, so he squirmed as he sat in the prosecution part of the gallery, glancing over at the defendant's side. Then he saw Rita's crazy boyfriend, Harvey, sitting right behind her, scowling.

Still shaking from the shock of the explosion, Ramsay grew more and more queasy as his time to testify drew near. He hoped that Harvey wouldn't appear and attack him some evening in the studio parking lot. He wished this Rita thing was over so he could focus on rebuilding the studio. The assistant DA, Marla Sanderson, had said her questions would be routine and obvious. The clerk called Ramsay's name and swore him in.

"How did you find the shortfall existed, Mr. Ramsay?" Ms. Sanderson asked.

"In the computer. My bank account didn't reconcile with my paid-off accounts receivable. Sometimes there's a little difference because a check hasn't cleared, but this difference was almost ten thousand dollars."

"Who had access to the incoming checks besides you?"

"Miss Scorpino."

"Could she have endorsed the incoming checks?"

"Yes. We had a stamp that we used," he said.

"And who had access to that stamp?"

"Only Miss Scorpino and I. There was a private place in the desk drawer."

After a cursory cross-examination, Ramsay left the stand and returned to the gallery. He was surprised to see Stan Devlin sitting on the prosecution side. An hour later, when the public defender called Rita, Ramsay was awestruck when she claimed that she had been hired by a group of photographers to undermine his studio with pranks like breaking glass, stealing money, and worse—a veritable conspiracy existed! The next witness called was Stan Devlin.

"So this conspiracy story is nonsense, you say?" Marla Sanderson asked him.

Devlin replied, "A lot of bunk. Rita told me one day how easy it would be to steal money from Marcus if you knew how to manipulate his system."

"And she implied that she knew how to do that?"

"Speculative!" called the young public defender.

"You may answer the question," the judge said.

"Oh, yes," Devlin said, "she sure did."

"That's not true!" Rita called.

"Order!" the judge said. "Mr. Darcy, please instruct your client on courtroom etiquette or I'll charge her with contempt."

"Yes, Your Honor," Mr. Darcy said. He leaned over and whispered to Rita.

Stan continued, "I've been a leader here in Orange County for twenty years and . . ."

Later that afternoon, Ms. Sanderson called Ramsay at the studio. "I think Stan Devlin's testimony will be the decisive blow."

The judge's decision only took a day. As Ramsay was setting aside several power packs that had been damaged beyond repair in the blast, the phone rang.

"Hi. Marla Sanderson here. I have good news. The judge came back with his decision."

"What is it?" he asked.

"Guilty," she said. "Devlin's testimony did it."

That night in his Irvine studio, Stan Devlin sat at his desk, celebrating with a warm beer. He wasn't in the mood to go home and listen to Rusty bark incessantly or Tracy giggle. In particular, he preferred not to listen to Joan drone on about how futile her job-seeking exploits were.

When Stan Devlin was twenty-five, he had worked hard to hone his photographic craft. Every day he woke up and headed to the studio. His brother, a dentist, had invented some instruments to make handling tiny objects easy. So Stan became the local expert at shooting "macro." In high-tech Orange County, that capability brought him multiple assignments shooting tiny chips and minuscule medical gadgets. If he was scheduled to shoot glassware—vials or test tubes—he merely employed a few strategically placed reflector cards on the set. He could plan on being paid fifteen hundred for the day. There were no questions or problems, and people always paid their bills on time. It was just another day of business growth in exciting Orange County.

Now the county had matured, and so had he. In order to shoot twice or three times a week, he had to bid against aggressive new photographers like Marcus Ramsay, who promised to perform styles of lighting Stan Devlin found different and strange. A serious decline in his business appeared imminent.

But he had taken action to prevent the changes that would hurt him. Not only had he destroyed his most significant new competitor, but he had avoided any incrimination by going to court and pointing the finger at Rita Scorpino. He had performed well as a star witness and long-standing community leader. He had saved himself by putting her away for years.

By enlisting the help of the volatile Art Zipper, a Vietnam demolition master, Stan knew he had pursued the right course—aggressive, but right.

While there would still be plenty of bidding battles on the horizon, there would not be a question as to who would lead the growing group of photographers in Orange County. Now Marcus Ramsay was out of it.

Laughably, as president of SIP, Ramsay would remain occupied trying to breathe life into the defunct shell of the organization that didn't stand a chance of refurbishment without Devlin's input. So the asshole MBA would be kept uselessly busy rebuilding—his studio and the photographers' organization.

Stan Devlin snickered. He felt only a twinge of guilt. On balance, things would be better for everyone. He could relax now. He sipped his warm beer and smiled.

11

Marcus Ramsay Photographic

During May and June, Marcus Ramsay sought to restore his blown-out studio but had trouble getting motivated. Thousands of dollars worth of irreparably damaged walls needed rebuilding and painting. With Tyler working at his side, Ramsay replaced whatever he could. Checks from clients slowed; the accounts seemed to be taking advantage of his vulnerability. Progress came to a halt.

All nine of his Norman strobe heads—flashes, at five hundred dollars each—had been sitting neatly by the back wall of the studio when the explosion occurred. Eight of his Norman power packs—at two thousand dollars each—had melted down from the intensity of the heat. His seven thousand dollar Sinar four-by-five P2 camera, once the pride of his life, now looked like a twisted, corroded monument. Some obscure lenses, tucked away in a special case, had survived the blast but were of little use without a camera.

By the looks of it, a small tactical nuclear weapon had decimated anything that resembled photo equipment. In fact, Marcus found it curious that the strike had been so surgical, as if it had been planned by minds aware of things photographic.

The insurance company, which Stan Devlin had recommended as the best for professional photographers, balked at a quick settlement because, they said, the blast seemed suspicious in nature. Their response quoted the fire department's report, which insinuated that there might have been owner involvement.

Despite Ramsay's daily calls to the office of the Tustin fire chief to reverse that impression, the wording of the original report remained. As June wore on, lack of an insurance settlement and the fire department's uppity attitude made Ramsay feel as if he had been convicted of fraud or worse.

During this time Marcus became deeply depressed. He couldn't fathom how another human being could have hurt his business so purposefully.

At Sylvia's suggestion he started seeing psychologist Cynthia Scott twice a week. She diagnosed his condition as acute posttraumatic stress disorder. She suggested that time would cure him of the persistent nightmares he had and the wariness he felt each time he walked into a parking lot at night. So he started routinely to leave the studio before sunset.

Each morning Ramsay arrived at eight and isolated himself in his studio office. There he fiddled on his Macintosh, fine-tuning the format of the SIP newsletter.

Later each day, Ramsay focused on building the organization's membership by calling nonmembers, personally inviting them to attend the next monthly meeting. He also called speakers who might make presentations to the group and asked for their help. With shooting impossible, he poured his heart into the SIP organization until three, when he left for home. Within a month his business came to a halt.

Meanwhile Sylvia became a comfort. Her daily chattering on the phone with prospects echoed from the front office. At lunchtime, Marcus and Sylvia would go up to Marge's sandwich shop. There Sylvia would talk soothingly about how he needed to heal his corporate wounds and accept them once and for all—truly mourning for them would make them vaporize. Ramsay listened to her coaching, but while it made some sense on an intellectual level, he had difficulty putting it into action.

Ramsay did little else. Day after day, week after week, the routine went on. Occasionally Tyler appeared to wash or paint another damaged area. Once in a while they hung, taped, and painted new sheetrock. Otherwise, the studio remained desolate and quiet—like an abandoned war zone.

The attendance for SIP meetings in June and July grew even though they were held at Chester's studio in the new Irvine Spectrum—not convenient because of the construction. Ramsay was surprised at how the clique seemed to dissipate into the crowd of newcomers. All of the attendees except Art Zipper and Stan Devlin subscribed to Ramsay's competitive price approach, too. At the August meeting, Devlin announced he had to leave early to take care of Tracy because, he said, Joan was busy preparing résumés and tapes. She had been fired from the Pacific Symphony.

To raise some cash, Ramsay held a *Ramsay on Light* seminar in early August. His profit was minimal because he used rented equipment. Many students complained about the studio resembling a construction zone and smelling of smoke.

The Cole Company took action regarding Ramsay's late rent payments, sending impersonal notices that warned of eviction. One day Marcus slumped to the management office to request that they lower his monthly rent until he got on his feet. Dana, the asset manager in charge of his suite, listened intently but only agreed to delay payment of his full obligation, plus penalties.

"Thanks a lot," he said, and he returned to his suite.

Every time he tried to reach Kathy, she was unavailable—protected by her assistants, Susan and JoAnn.

One day, as Marcus Ramsay fiddled at his Mac, the doorbell rang. A minute later he felt someone staring at him. It was Kathy.

"I heard what happened," she said. "The bomb."

"You came rushing over, I noticed," he said. "Kathy, it's been months!"

"I'm sorry; I've had my hands full at work."

"Man, not even a note or a call?"

She looked bored. "I did take on the role of breadwinner in Texas, didn't I? If it wasn't for me, you wouldn't have had *any* funding to start this photo thing."

"Kathy, with or without me in your life, you would've done the same thing," he said. "Pursue your dreams in the Abyss. So, don't claim any credit for putting yourself out on my behalf."

"If it wasn't for me . . . ," she continued.

"Kathy, let me ask you something. Did you ever really care about the photo business?"

She stood there silently, hands on hips.

"It was always a bother to you, wasn't it?" he asked angrily.

"I'm going to go," she said.

"Why? It's true, isn't it?"

"Marcus, I came to see if I could help."

"Sure, like the day you bailed on me—or the evening you ate dinner with me while you were planning to dump me?"

"That was just unfortunate timing."

"Oh, right. Listen, I don't need your damn money. That was never the kind of support I've needed from you."

"As far as I'm concerned, it was." Like a little general, with hands propped behind her back, Kathy turned and marched out.

Ramsay sat, stunned in his desk chair. After he heard the front door close, he cradled his head in his hands and cried.

Earlier in the summer Jessica had wandered from Ramsay, too. Before the blast they had talked weekly, but he was lucky if they talked once a month now. They never had that third swim. The few times Ramsay saw her, she had just finished completing assignments for other photographers. One afternoon she stopped by his studio.

"Hi," he said.

"You look awful; like you haven't slept or shaved for a week," she said. "Are you okay?"

"Did you stop by to criticize my hygiene?"

"I'm sorry, but you've always been so resilient. Now, nothing."

"So?" he said.

"You don't want to plan a swim, do you?" she asked.

"Nah."

"Figures," she muttered.

After a few minutes of silence, she sighed, crept out to her Geo Metro, and putted away. Since the explosion, that was the longest conversation they had.

One night Marcus Ramsay slept restlessly. Then, exhausted, he slipped into a deep sleep and had a vivid, strange dream.

A glowing phoenix stepped from the burning fire before him. It climbed out of the flames unscathed, and made its way up to Ramsay, who lay there charred and smoky. The bird stopped and stood on a pile of rocks next to him.

Ramsay wore only tattered clothes. His face was filthy, his hair singed, and his body bruised.

The bird said, "You have made a difficult journey and have been injured. It appears you cannot continue on your quest."

"Yes, I think my journey is over. I will no longer be able to follow my dreams."

"Rise, sir," the bird said. "You feel weak, but you have only been beaten down temporarily. The smoke that surrounds you makes it difficult for you to see."

At once, Ramsay recalled his seminars, when he talked about *seeing the light*. "So, if I look through this wall of smoke, will I see my future?" he asked.

The glowing bird had a faint, maternal smile. "Yes, it is that simple. You only have to look. I shall offer you a way to see, and you must take it. Believing will create the energy you need."

Ramsay woke from his dream sweating profusely, his body feeling heavy, like he had slept for days. As the day wore on, he remembered the details and wrote them down.

Later, in what started as a bland phone conversation with Jessica, she listened to his story of the dream. She said it sounded like something Suzanne would tell her.

"What is she, a New Age fanatic?" Ramsay asked.

"Does she believe in the power of crystals?"

"No, she just exists on a different plane than the rest of us."

"I'm just confused. What does dreaming about giant birds have to do with my life?"

"Well, you shoot beautiful photographs, right?"

"So?"

"And you can't move on from your hassles?"

"Yes."

"Then, your dream is saying that you are ready to rise from the ashes like a phoenix."

"No offense, but that sounds like a bunch of bull."

"But," Jessica said, "according to Suzanne, that bull is just positive energy you can't ignore. Your energy can be so positive it will overcome the negative."

"Jessica? Do you exist in my negative or positive realm?"

"I don't know. But I will say that when I'm feeling negative Suzanne's not necessarily the one I want to visit."

"Why is that?"

"She'll just try to bring me back to a more positive state. She is instantly in touch with my vulnerable self and knows how my energy can be converted from grief to celebration. It's quite incredible how she heals."

"Sounds like a magic woman," Ramsay said.

"Could be. Hmm. Listen, I have to go. Suddenly I'm not feeling real good." She cleared her throat.

"Are you okay, Jessica?"

The phone clicked.

A week later, as August was about to turn into September, Sylvia said, "That dream means you should keep fighting back, Marcus. Don't ignore it."

"But," Marcus said, "it was only a dream."

"Look. If you dreamt it, it came out of your brain, right? The idea of recovering from this garbage must be in you."

"I agree," Tyler said. "I'm getting tired of the dismal attitude around the studio. Maybe you ought to have your sensors up for the good stuff and it'll come your way. Before the blast, things looked pretty good, right? Maybe all that can come back. Bev always says, 'Have your sensors up.' I think she's right. It makes a difference."

When Ramsay returned to his office after lunch, Ramsay pulled out his sepia-toned photograph of old Sycamore Studios before the fire. Since then Donald had rebuilt the place in a new location and it had thrived for ten years. Ramsay waved the photo and decided it was time to raise his sensors and welcome a new future.

"Marcus Ramsay?" an attractive Asian lady said as she glided into Ramsay's office the next afternoon.

He looked up. "What is it?"

In a choppy cadence, the Asian woman chattered about how she had started the day so badly. "Hopefully, this call will be better," she said.

He motioned for her to sit in a chair on the other side of his desk.

"Thank you, Mr. Ramsay."

"Sorry for the smell," he said. "I was bombed several months ago."

"I know," she said and smiled.

"You do? Miss?"

"Wong. Desiree Wong. Marcus, have you ever heard of AIEF?"

"No, I can't afford to contribute—"

"No, I'm not about selling anything. I'm from the Orange County Advertising Industry Emergency Fund," she said. "We can help you recover from this mess."

"Like how? The insurance hasn't come through. It might not, ever."

"AIEF can help." For the next hour Desiree wrote on her yellow legal pad as Ramsay answered questions about his loss: the extent of the fire, what insurance covered, the semicooperation of the fire department—all the details. She explained that AIEF was an organization supported by voluntary contributions from the advertising industry in Orange County and that, should any of its members need to recover from a catastrophic loss, the organization would help—the AIEF was a Red Cross for the advertising industry.

"Really, you'll help me? That's hard to believe," he said.

"James Honeybear gave us your name," Desiree said.

"Wow, Jim came through for me."

"He was really concerned."

"He always seemed so cool. Pleasant but cool."

"James asked us to look into this. I promised him I'd pay personal attention to your case," she said.

"Really? They'll help cover part of my losses?" Ramsay said. He waved his hands around.

"No, Marcus." She smiled. "All of your losses will be covered—as long as our board agrees. This case is a clear one. So, congratulations! I bet you'll be back in business soon."

"Far out." Ramsay jumped up, smiled, and shook Desiree's hand energetically.

She laughed.

"This is unbelievable," he said.

"I'll probably be getting a check to you within a week. Then you can start your rebuild."

Desiree continued, "That's why I love my job so much. I see so many smiles. I feel like James Beresford Tipton on that old TV show *The Millionaire*."

"Beresford is Honeybear's real name, you know?" he said.

"I'm pleased we could work together to help you out."

"Man, I'm glad you stopped by today," Ramsay said as he ushered Desiree to the front door. She started walking across the parking lot.

He called after her, "Even the smell, right?"

"What?"

"The smoke smell. It's everywhere. Covered by the AIEF, right? Drywall, paint."

"All of it. Relax, Mr. Ramsay. You'll be back in business again soon." Desiree got into her car, waved, and drove away.

"Just like a phoenix," he said.

12

Marcus Ramsay Photographic

By late September, after a busy month of reconstruction, Ramsay was looking forward to reopening his studio.

"It looks great!" Tyler said as he studied the new walls, equipment, and tools.

"You know, I think I should have the next SIP meeting here," Ramsay said. "Show off the place."

"Sure. It looks great! New stereo system, tools, and equipment—it's beautiful."

Ramsay smiled. "You ain't seen nothin' yet, Tyler."

"What else do you have in mind?" Tyler said.

"Don't Fall Behind," Ramsay said.

"What?"

"My next promotion to celebrate the studio's reopening. I'll fax a promotion to clients offering a five-hundred-dollar-a-day discount."

"Devlin'll hate that—he'll say you're undercutting him. Especially since you share some of his clients."

"Now we're going to beat him at his own game."

"You don't want to piss him off, do you?"

"What could Stan Devlin do to me that hasn't been done already?"

The crowd streamed into Marcus Ramsay's rebuilt studio for the October SIP meeting. Everybody studied the freshly painted white walls and listened to the sound of the Eagles as they played on the new stereo system.

The crowd gabbed excitedly as they sat in their seats. More folding chairs had to be set up to accommodate the increased number of attendees. A few people even had to stand.

Ken Potter, who had been in the reception area taking the money, dodged through the studio and hurried up to Ramsay. "Marcus, at ten bucks a head, we have over a thousand bucks in the treasury now!"

"That's great."

"Flush for the first time I can remember," Potter said and scratched his beard. "Probably came out to see the program tonight." He walked away.

When Tyler walked up, Ramsay looked around the studio, teeming with photographers. "You seen Devlin?" Ramsay asked.

"Over there, leaning against that pillar. Looks sort of pissed."

"Probably envious he never pulled in this many. He's so insecure."

"Where's Art?" Tyler said.

"Guess he couldn't make it."

As the crowd settled down, James Honeybear walked up to the podium, his glass of Chardonnay held high. "Before we start, I want to remind you that we have five reasons to celebrate tonight."

They hushed.

"First, SIP has grown to over a hundred general members and we've added another ten trade sponsors. Second, the programs are more interesting; and third, our newsletter's better than ever—full of facts and photo tips."

The group applauded.

His voice boomed. "Fourth, for the first time, we have women shooters in the group!"

More applause.

"There's more." Honeybear toasted. "Tonight we celebrate the reopening of Marcus Ramsay's studio. His rebound has been an inspiration to us all."

The group cheered.

"SIP has Marcus to thank for all of all his outstanding work for the organization, too. You've really put us on the map, Marcus. Congratulations on the studio—it's beautiful."

James toasted Ramsay again.

"Speech!" they called.

As Ramsay walked to the front, he brushed by Stan Devlin, making a beeline toward the front door.

13

California Pizza Kitchen, Encino, California

The following week, Jessica and Marcus met at the California Pizza Kitchen near her house.

"So how was the meeting?" she asked.

"Great. Except Devlin made a scene when he left in a huff."

"Why?"

"That's what I wondered," he said. "I hope he hasn't gotten wind of my next promotion."

"Another one?"

"Yeah. I'll call this one *Don't Fall Behind*," Ramsay said with a smile. "It's planned to coincide with the Monday after we set the clocks back."

"Cool. Tell me about it."

"I'll be offering a five-hundred-dollar discount to my clients via fax. Since he and I share some clients, he's bound to hear about it from them. He may even lose some of them to me."

"That SAP board meeting's coming up soon, right?"

"Yeah."

"Stan'll bitch, I bet," she said.

"Yeah."

"Don't trust him, Marcus."

"That's what I understand," he said.

She paused. "I heard he's the point man for the campaign to make things tough on you."

"That was Rita's claim, but Stan denied it outright in court."

"I wouldn't be surprised if he had something to do with the bombing."

"Why do you think so?"

"I've just heard stuff from other photographers and models."

"Well," he laughed. "After next week, they won't be able to find me. I'm heading out to the Grand Canyon on a little vacation for a few days."

"Really?" She smiled.

"Why, what is it?"

"Oh . . . nothing," she said and stared into space.

"Well, then," he said, "is the South Rim better than the North Rim?"

"You'd like the South Rim," Jessica said. "And don't call it *the* Grand Canyon. Remember, the rangers omit the *the* to avoid making it a generic descriptor."

"Just Grand Canyon, then."

"That's it," she said. "Maybe you can work on some healing with my sister."

"Yeah. Kathy said she thinks my anger from the past is fueling my new future. Sylvia implied the same thing. She thinks I need to mourn—get cleansed of my grief."

"Sounds right. Suzanne can help."

"Maybe. I think I'm open to something like that now."

"I thought you were."

After dinner they drove back to Jessica's place. She walked Marcus to his Jeep. They stood under a lone streetlight to say good-bye.

"Marcus?" she asked.

"Yeah?"

"Please hug me. I need a good one."

He cuddled her. "What's wrong, Jessica?" He could feel her tremble. "You're shaking. Cold?"

She sighed. "Mmm. You hug the best. I wish you could always hug me. I've been so lonely."

"What's wrong, Jesse?" he asked. They rocked as they hugged.

"The doctor was right. I need to find people I can love and who'll love me back. I can't go around moping."

"What doctor? Why have you been moping?"

"It's a long story. But now I know what I have to do to be happy."

"What is that?"

"Just be who I've always wanted to be," she said.

Ramsay cupped her cheeks in both his hands. "Sounds right, Jesse."

"I like it when you call me Jesse. Is there a chance for us to be together?"

"Jessica, at times I feel close to you, but I have to admit that when I do, it's like you're the sister I never had. I don't know about any romance."

As tears appeared in her eyes, he gently kissed her on her cheek. He had never seen her cry. "What's wrong, Jesse?" he asked.

"Sometimes you make me melt, Marcus," she said. "I hate bickering with you. Shoot, my life is so screwed up."

"Don't worry. Everything'll work out." He kissed her again, then started to get in his car. "I guess I have to get the Jeep ready—oil change, lube, all that—for my trip to

Grand Canyon. Maybe I'll even see your sister," he said.

"You will," she sniffled. "When you going?"

"Next weekend. I'm bringing my camera to shoot some landscapes."

"It can be a little hazy there sometimes," Jessica said. "Do you have to go now, Marcus? I need you."

Ramsay smiled. "You'll be fine. I'll take a nice shot of Suzanne if I see her, okay?"

"Thanks. Say hi to her from me, okay? She hangs out mornings at the Watchtower, down the road from the El Tovar Lodge—that's where I recommend staying."

"El Tovar."

"I'm sure she'll share some deep thoughts with you. She always does—Native American stuff." Jessica waved a tiny good-bye as she turned away.

She turned back. "I'm her kachina, you know?"

"What's that?" he asked.

"Someday you'll understand. If I talk to her, I'll tell her you're coming."

"I assume I'll recognize her." He laughed.

She smiled. "No doubt."

A week later Marcus Ramsay drove to the Jolly Roger restaurant on Dyer Road where the SIP board regularly met. He had made it a habit to arrive early at the meetings, pass out the agenda, and have a peaceful cup of tea while he waited for the other board members. Then they would typically wander in, eat breakfast, and discuss the details on the agenda. As they sipped their second cup of coffee or tea, they would plan the next general membership meeting and discuss other issues. By this time Stan Devlin would undoubtedly have heard about Ramsay's *Fall Behind* promotion and grumble enviously.

This morning Ramsay expected laurels for having rejuvenated the organization. Last week's general membership meeting at his studio had been so successful that the accolades were already slipping through the grapevine. So they would undoubtedly resurface at this meeting—he was looking forward to them.

Earlier that morning, while he was shaving, he had drifted to Sylvia's advice over the previous months. Maybe now it was time to cast away the corporate hurt that had dragged him down for so long. Since he had recovered from the blast, he was ready to shed his defeats and start anew.

As he pulled into the Jolly Roger parking lot, Marcus imagined the board congratulating him heartily and Stan Devlin moping. He parked near the door and strolled into the group's normal meeting room.

Marcus was shocked.

The entire board was sitting there at a table, speaking in a low grumble. Ten sober eyes were staring at him. From the looks of their spent coffee cups and cigarette butts, they'd been there for a while. Stan Devlin sat at the center of the table, à la Jesus in *The Last Supper*. Devlin smirked at Ramsay as he shuffled a stack of white papers.

"Stan, what is this about?" Ramsay asked.

Devlin spoke: "Marcus, we came early for a reason." He tapped the stack of papers on the table. "Just sit down."

Elise, one of the two women elected to the board, spoke first: "Maybe we should let you start, Stan, since you called us together."

"What's going on?" Ramsay asked.

"We've met to discuss this *Fall Behind* shit," Devlin said.

"What about it?" Ramsay asked.

"My clients received these faxes from you," he charged.

"So?" Ramsay asked.

"This promotion offers a discount of five hundred dollars," Devlin sneered.

"And?"

"To *my* clients!" Devlin said. The clinking of coffee cups stopped.

Shivering slightly, Ramsay said, "Stan, who here hasn't worked for Backman, SMS, or Conroy?"

"You're trying to steal my clients by discounting!"

"Not long ago, you went on the record, Stan, saying we should all raise our rates to fifteen hundred a day. Right?"

"Of course?"

"Do you agree with that?" Ramsay asked.

"That's hardly news."

"Well, I know for a fact that you arbitrarily lowered your rates to win a bid. You've been deliberately encouraging all of us to quote high numbers so that you can bid low and win the assignments."

The other board members looked at Stan.

"That's not true," he said and cleared his throat.

"I can prove it," Ramsay said.

"That's not the point of this meeting." Devlin slammed the table, then held up the stack of papers. "If you're going to be the president of SIP you have to be above all this price-cutting stuff."

"Devlin, you've always been out for yourself, haven't you? This kangaroo court is just another example. I've even heard that you and Art were involved in bombing my studio."

Stan flinched. "That's nonsense, Ramsay." Devlin sipped his coffee and looked at the others. "Just more MBA bullshit!"

"Well, what do the rest of you have to say?" Ramsay asked.

Each member of the board looked around, everywhere but at Ramsay.

"That figures," Ramsay muttered, and rose. He stormed out, not looking back. The rumble of SIP voices faded, and the clinking of cups jingled in his ears as he flung open the front door of the Jolly Roger. He stomped into the parking lot. He had overcome some impossible ordeals over the previous year, but this political maneuver was so reminiscent of his corporate debacle that it tore open that old wound.

He opened his car door, climbed in, started up his car, and swerved through the tiny Jolly Roger parking lot.

"That asshole!" Ramsay fumed, beet red. As he drove back to the studio, he composed a resignation letter that he planned to fax to all of the board members: "If the group's going to return to an ignorant price-fixing mentality, I hereby resign as president of SIP."

He flashed back to his dismissal in Texas, where he had been flying high and was undermined by the ruthless lying of someone's incompetence—this episode was of the same genre. Salt was pouring into that wound.

14

Eastbound Route 40, San Bernardino County, California

Still stinging from the surprise at the SIP board meeting, Marcus drove north on the 5 freeway, then east on 91 to Route 15, then north again, then straight east on Route 40 toward Grand Canyon. He had packed as little as possible, haphazardly throwing two changes of clothes into the scuffed avocado-colored suitcase that he had originally gotten for his honeymoon.

He rolled down his window and let the dusty, dry air swish his hair this way and that. He was rattled, but the wind rushing through his hair and whirring past his ears diffused his anger.

"It just isn't fair," he kept saying. He felt the same as he had after getting fired—completely violated.

To distract himself, he pictured the next few days. He planned to stay at the El Tovar Lodge on the South Rim, where Jessica said the views of the canyon would be best.

Still suppressing his anger as he sped east, he contemplated the idea of screwing the photography to return to marketing, this time without Kathy as his spouse. You never knew what or who to believe in the photography profession, he figured. The hypocrisy was so rampant—it was a career hardly worth pursuing.

Slowly, over the course of the trip, Marcus cooled down. *Can't the rest of them see through Devlin's bullshit?*

Ramsay thought. He fumed as he pictured Devlin smirking after the meeting—the man had finally gotten his way.

Ramsay rolled on. After an hour he passed through the Ponderosas at the entrance of the Kaibab National Forest. Soon the signs appeared announcing Grand Canyon National Park.

As he climbed out of his Jeep in the visitors' area to stretch, Ramsay looked at the immense canyon in shadow. He figured he would have to wait until the next morning for some good shots.

He walked into the El Tovar Lodge and passed its large rock fireplace. He checked into his room, showered, and took a nap.

He woke feeling relaxed and went down to the first-floor dining room for dinner. Bordered by walls of exposed lots, the room was elegantly lit by rectangular stained-glass lamps—simple and rustic.

A waitress with a friendly smile approached. He smiled back. She recited the specials.

"I'll have the filet, medium rare."

"Yes, sir," the waitress said.

"Say, miss, do you know the rangers who work here?" he asked.

"Who are you looking for?"

"Dasher's the last name. Suzanne."

"Sounds familiar. I'll ask around," she said.

Minutes later, as Ramsay sipped on his merlot and ate a small salad, he noticed a group of servers gathered at the kitchen door. They eyed him suspiciously as they talked.

What the hell is that for? he wondered.

The waitress returned. "Here's your food." Her friendly smile had been replaced by an uppity attitude.

She deposited Ramsay's dinner harshly and walked away.

After Ramsay finished his entrée, he slowly ate a hot fudge sundae and was determined not to succumb to the salvos of disapproving glances. He concluded these earthy types must hate anyone who looked like he might be from LA.

When he finished his sundae, he rose and glanced defiantly at the cold stares. Minutes later, in his room, he wondered why the manner of the place had shifted so suddenly.

He got ready for bed. The mattress wasn't much better than the hospitality: hard and cold.

Marcus figured he'd take Jessica's advice and rise early to shoot the sunrise from the Watchtower. From that perspective, it would shine against the west and north walls of the canyon. Maybe he'd run into Suzanne there.

Later that night back in Orange County, Stan Devlin sat in his studio office. He was lightly tending to his books as he relished the completeness of his victory over Marcus Ramsay. Devlin had obliterated the man's studio months before with the help of Art Zipper. Devlin had known all along Art would be up for a heavy action against Ramsay should it become necessary. He had come through.

Devlin sipped on his beer. Marcus Ramsay, the MBA bean counter, had rebuilt SIP and taken it over by making a few phone calls to some useless newcomers and even women. But he got his! The chickenshit had crumbled under a little political maneuvering.

Stan Devlin had finally reestablished his position as undisputed warlord of all south Orange County photographers. He sat in his desk chair and puffed out his chest. The position had been his birthright all along.

Wait a second! What will happen now that the MBA bastard is gone? Devlin wondered. *Will I be able to manage a new era of photography: competitive pricing, fancy lighting, and digital shooting?*

Stan looked up. He thought he heard a reverberating cracking noise from his darkened studio.

He walked toward his office door and hurried around the corner. As he yanked open the studio door, he ran into a large, vaguely familiar-looking man with wild hair. He must have gained entry through the unlocked front door.

"Can I help you?" Devlin asked.

Without saying a world, the man rushed him. He grabbed Devlin's shirt and threw him against the studio wall. He laughed like he was playing some demented game. "You put my baby away, you asshole."

"What?" Stan pushed back, but the man's strength was too great. He flung Devlin into the studio door.

"What the hell?" Devlin said, panting as he hit the wall.

The man grunted and laughed. He stomped toward Devlin, grabbed him by the shirt, and repeatedly tossed him against the wall, which dented each time Stan was thrown against it. After three hits, the man yanked him down the hall and into the bathroom.

"Wait!" Devlin yelped.

The large man cornered him and pummeled him with a succession of punches to the head and body.

When the man reached for his belt, Devlin recognized him as Rita's boyfriend. A second later Devlin felt a sharp object penetrate his gut. As he grabbed for his stomach, blood spurted through his hands. He felt jabs of pain again and again.

Stan choked, "You can take . . . money."

"Fuck you!" the man grunted. "You deserve this, Devlin. You took her from me and now you'll pay!"

"Please!" Devlin called. The pain floated away. Soon he saw vague shadows and heard only muffled sounds.

15

Grand Canyon

Saturday when he woke, Ramsay was surprised he had slept at all, the bumps had made his bedding so uncomfortable. His back throbbed and shoulder muscles felt like he had spent the night sleeping on the ground.

He shaved, slung his camera bag over his shoulder, and walked to the restaurant, where he grabbed a quick cup of hot tea. Afterward, he headed down the dusty, rocky road leading to the Watchtower, where Jessica said he could get some great morning shots. As he glanced to his left, he saw the morning light glow on the north and west facets of the canyon wall, miles away. A surprisingly cool, stout breeze blew at him as he looked around for families, foreigners, and buses, but none had arrived to stir the early hour.

He entered the Watchtower, a lighthouse-shaped building with a small shop on the first floor. He went through a marked door and climbed an earthen, circular staircase. On the higher floors he found Hopi art, much of it hunting and fertility symbols. Near the top, Ramsay metered the light as it streamed through the thin rectangular windows around the tower's perimeter. He took out his camera and framed some shots to see which view he liked most.

He looked out a window as the sun crept across the

canyon. Shadows formed as the light hit the jagged sandstone relief on the gorge, giving the opposite canyon wall a sculpted appearance. He relaxed with his can of Coke and, when he stood perfectly still, could see the shadow from the emerging sunlight as it slipped over the rock.

Then he heard footsteps echo as someone entered the stairwell and climbed the staircase. In seconds, a tanned woman with bushy, auburn hair and sparkling eyes appeared. "Hello," an outdoorsy version of Jessica said. "You're Marcus, right?"

"Yeah. Suzanne? My God. You do look like Jessica, don't you?" he said. "Except for your hair and that tan." She wore an ivory gauze blouse, faded denim cut-offs, and old hiking boots. "Where's the uniform?"

"I have the weekend plus Monday and Tuesday off, so I'm doing the civilian thing."

"In this light your coloring is spectacular, Suzanne—the auburn in your hair, your tan; they really blend well with the earthen hues in here." Ramsay raised his 35mm camera. "Would you mind?"

"Guess not," she said shyly.

'It'll be okay. Just follow my cues."

"I'm not used to this. Sort of fulfills a fantasy—you know, modeling. Like Jesse."

"Just stand over there," Ramsay said.

"Here?" Suzanne's talk was slower, smoother, and lower than Jessica's nasal banter.

Ramsay reached into his camera bag and replaced his 50mm lens with the 100mm. For an hour, as the morning light shone through the little windows, Ramsay took different views of Suzanne.

The shot that he particularly liked was one of her

perched in a window with the illuminated canyon in the background. Her tan blended perfectly with the earthen walls and the morning light that reflected from them. The rays bounced off her blouse and filled her face. The whites of her eyes and her teeth appeared opalescent.

They talked so comfortably that Ramsay found himself wanting to be closer to her. He was able to talk to Suzanne like he had known her a hundred years.

"Is this okay, Marcus?" she asked. She gently flowed from pose to pose, waving her hands and bending her wrists gently. "Jessica has it made. This modeling is so easy."

"You look like you could've done this before. Hand modeling is much harder than this free-flowing stuff, though," he said. "What Jessica does takes tremendous patience and concentration."

"You know, when we talk on the phone, Jesse always bubbles about you," she said.

"Jessica's very nice. Challenging in a way. Sometimes a little too confrontational."

"Confrontational?"

"It can be irritating at times," he said. "Why don't we try a few shots over there?"

"You like her, don't you?" Suzanne asked.

"I guess." He stopped and thought. "In a quirky sort of way."

"Why quirky?" She crinkled her brow.

"Well, we have trouble getting along once in a while." He shrugged and continued shooting. "Actually, sort of often."

"How?" she asked.

"Oh, it's silly. We bicker a lot. Then I get angry at her."

"Hmm. She's like that with me, too," Suzanne said. "It's just her way. She sees things in black-and-white. But her fixed view of the world confirms how insecure she is. She prompts everyone around her to buy into her thinking. She's always struggling to build her self-esteem and really depends on what others think."

"Man, that's exactly it." He put his camera down as she stopped moving. "I couldn't have said it any better. It's not just my imagination, then. Is Jessica a little crazy?" He laughed as he walked up close to her, propped her hair on her shoulder, sniffed it, and closed his eyes for a second. "Nice fragrance," he said.

"It's my shampoo. A friend of mine makes it from scratch, lots of herbs."

"Nice. So, do you think she's a little wacky?" he asked.

"Jessica? Hmm." Suzanne looked at the ground in thought. "Maybe you could call it that. I think it's mainly because she's so smart. The smarter you are, the crazier you seem to everyone who's not as smart. Right?"

"True. I've thought that very thing about her. You can tell she's brilliant," Ramsay said. "Okay, now let's shoot some over by this window. You're doing great, Suzanne."

"I know Jessica likes you a lot," she said, "but I don't think she'd mind if we hang around."

"Nice pose, Suzanne! Sure, I guess we can spend some time together, try some of that healing bit."

"You aren't married, are you?" she asked.

"Not anymore. I still feel like it, though." The split was Kathy's idea. It sure happened suddenly."

"Shook you up I bet."

"Yeah."

"You were married for a long time, then?"

He shrugged his shoulders. "Ten years."

"Do you feel okay hanging out with me?" she asked.

"Sure. This is the first time in a long time I've felt free. Maybe because I know Jessica, I feel like I've known you forever, too. It's so natural being with you."

"Good." She flashed a smile. "Say, want to come over and see my place? Have a little tea?"

"Sure. You know, once Jessica told me that a person's place is really an elaborate piece of art that reflects who they are."

"She told me that, too."

"It's true, I guess," he said.

"A reasonable thought."

As the sun rose through the morning, Ramsay shot several rolls of film. After three hours, Ramsay and Suzanne walked down the stony road to her motel room just outside the park.

"So you live here?" he asked as they entered. She walked over to the spartan kitchen and poured two sweaty glasses of iced tea.

"It suffices. They give me an employee discount," she said, "since I'm a senior ranger. It's better than the cabins in the park they give to the rookies. Those are hot boxes."

"I like the southwestern look and adobe walls, but this is a bit plain for my tastes," he said.

"I like it simple," she said. "It helps me live in the present, you know." She handed him a glass of tea.

He nodded.

"Jesse told me about some job loss you went through, too," she said.

"Yeah, it was a surprise, like my divorce," he said.

"Sounds awful. I bet they still get to you from two angles: anger and pain."

"I guess." He shrugged.

"You know, I might be able to help you cast those stones away forever."

He looked up. "How can you tell the pain is still there?"

She smiled. "Let's just say I know."

Ramsay put his glass down and stood up. "You and Sylvia are both saying I need to mourn. How can you both see it?"

"Sylvia?"

"My studiomate."

"Well . . . it's probably obvious to us," she said, "because we're not as close to the pain as you are."

"By the way, can I have some more tea?"

She filled his glass. "Marcus, maybe I can help you heal. I've helped others face their pain and see beyond it."

"That's what Jessica said."

"I even helped an old boyfriend face his grief when his mother died. It was awful. He lived with the pain for months. Then I took him to a special place that his people kept for healing."

"Special place?"

"Yes, a sacred Native American place. It's wonderfully cleansing to go there. Their ceremonies make it very special."

"What ceremonies?"

"For cleansing, healing—to rid you of your pain. They're based on old traditions and some new ideas. You should try doing some of these things while you're here. You up for it?"

"If you really think it'll help." He hung his head.

"I bet you've gone to shrinks, right?"

"Yeah."

"Well, this is the same idea, just from another culture. It'll help you let it all go." She walked up to him and brushed his hair back on both sides of his face. "Let's try tomorrow—the weather'll be perfect. Okay?" she asked. "You're tired. Why don't we hit the sack. You can sleep on the cot. There are sheets in the cabinet. Use that pillow. We can go to the site in the morning light. You'll be able to get some wonderful shots of the canyon, too—but only of the canyon, not the special place."

"Why not?"

"It's sacred," she said.

"Got it." He nodded.

She leaned up and gave him a peck on the cheek. "Sweet dreams, Marcus. I'm glad we met." Then she spun around, grabbed an old T-shirt from under the pillow on her bed, and walked into the tiny bathroom.

As she ran water in the bathroom, he took off his jeans and settled into the cot.

16

Grand Canyon

"Want some tea, Marcus?" Suzanne asked in a low, smooth voice in the early-morning darkness.

"Do you have English Breakfast?" he whispered, barely awake.

"Sure," she said. She pulled out a small tray of different kinds of tea.

She wore a different peasant blouse from the day before. It was also gauze, but it had a finely embroidered multicolored pattern across the neckline and hung slightly off her well-formed shoulders.

Ramsay pulled the blankets around him. He sipped on his tea.

"It's still early," she said, "but we need to head out to the healing place before it gets hot."

Ramsay sat up and stretched in bed. "That ceremony bit is for real, huh?"

"Oh, yes. Today will be a very important day," she said.

"Sounds mysterious."

Suzanne glared at him. "Marcus, you can't joke about this."

"Sorry," he said.

"This kind of healing may be unfamiliar to you, but it is potent and very real." She reached for his tea cup. "Here, let me pour you another." She brewed him a new cup. "And you have to trust me unconditionally."

"I trust you," he said. "I do."

"You think you do. Now you will begin to see what trust really means." She handed him a small worn leather loincloth. "Put this on under your pants instead of those bikinis."

"That looks old."

"It's an ancient ceremonial garment."

After Ramsay dressed, he slung his 35mm camera bag over his shoulder. He waited as Suzanne packed her backpack with various implements.

They left the motel room. As they walked along a trail into the park, Suzanne spoke more of the healing process. "So, what I do is actually go into you," she said, "and see what's ailing you. In this case, it would be the remnants of the pain from your divorce, job loss, rejection from the photo community, or all three. It could just as well be a tumor or other physical problem. To me they are very much the same."

"What do you actually see?" he asked.

"It depends; maybe it's more like *feel*. I will speak to you as I enter you; then I will know. I hope you are ready."

As they walked along the trail, they gazed out at the canyon.

"It sounds a bit strange, and I admit I have a cynical side," he said.

Suddenly she stopped, turned, and put her hand on his chest. "Wait. Last night you agreed that you need help with all this bad stuff."

"I guess I do," he said. "At least, everybody keeps telling me stuff."

"Listen, Marcus. You must totally trust me and leave your doubts behind." She reached up and gently stroked his face. "That is the only way I can help you—and I do think I can."

He closed his eyes and sighed. "Okay. If you put it like that, I won't joke around anymore."

"Listen, Marcus. I don't even know if you're ready," she said. "I'm guessing you might not be."

"Really?"

"I'll only be able to tell when we get to the special place and start the ceremony."

They continued on the trail as it passed the Tovar Lodge, then turned left and followed a thinner path that led into the canyon. It was partially obscured by heaps of dry bushes, which Suzanne pushed aside.

"Does this one go to the bottom of the canyon?" he asked.

"Yes, but after a while we'll leave it," she said. As the trail became steeper, she continued to push aside heaps of dried bushes until there were none.

"Man. That's a little easier," he called to her. "This is so steep, I bet this is tough walking back out."

She stopped for a second, took a swig of water, and looked back at him. "It takes about twice as much time to get out as it does to get in—that's the rule we use. That's why I brought so much water." As Suzanne walked, she waddled slightly from the weight of four water bottles attached to her Velcro-covered belt.

She waved her hands in the air and talked in a melodic voice about how everything was one, having come from the great embodiment billions of years ago.

Then she shifted gears and told the story of a little

Native American girl.

"Shanna's mother sat her down one morning and said, 'Baby, after you grow old you will become tired. One day your spirit will leave and fly away.'"

"'What happens then, Mother?'" Shanna asked.

"'Don't worry, baby. You will go to a magic place no one's ever seen. You will come back as a kachina doll so you can live forever and be honored by your ancestors. In that way you will become part of Father Spirit.'"

"That's beautiful, Suzanne," Marcus said.

"Native Americans are way ahead spiritually," she said. "They have always accepted the notion of oneness, and in some tribes young children are taught the kachina tales so they grow up accepting death as part of life. They learn that their souls will fly endlessly on the wings of others."

"That's so cool," he said.

"Isn't it?" she said.

"You tell the story in such a compelling manner. I feel like I'm learning with Shanna."

"Through storytelling, the truth can become acceptable. It is easier to have faith." She shook her head and snickered. "It's amazing how ignorant our society has become."

Ramsay nodded. "You know, Suzanne, I've always been attracted to ideas like these, but my friends think I'm crazy."

"It might sound silly when you compare it to our traditional Puritanical way of thinking. But our way would've seemed pretty outrageous to the average Native American years ago."

"I can see that. The Shanna story sounds so rational,

like it's part of some great plan."

"It is." Suzanne stopped and sipped some water. "Here, have another swig. Keeps you hydrated."

He took the water bottle. "Mmm."

He gave the bottle back to her, then they continued down the trail.

She said, "The one great belief we all share is love. Think about it: It is our feeble attempt to be close to each other, to regain total restoration of the oneness. But because we use love so conditionally, we never experience its true power. We don't allow ourselves to experience its freedom. Instead, we only occasionally glimpse it. When we get it, we are enraptured by it."

Suzanne stopped, sipped more water, and stared at the precipitous fall-off. She continued to walk, but now a little closer to the cliff wall.

"Here." Minutes later Suzanne pushed aside some brush and exposed a slim crack in the rock. "Come on, Marcus, this way."

Ramsay followed her as she slipped into the nearly vertical two-foot-wide crevasse. Marcus and Suzanne felt their way through the dark passageway, often scraping their bodies or heads on unseen jagged rocks. After fifty feet or so, the tunnel curved to the right. Morning light spilled through a slightly thinner opening.

"We're here, Marcus. Just squeeze yourself through," she said. Suzanne held her breath as she crawled toward the light.

Ramsay followed, pushing aside loose gravel and clutching his camera. He righted himself and rubbed his eyes as he climbed out of the crevasse. He stretched, then looked to his left at a spectacular view of the canyon. "Wow." In front of him a thirty-by-thirty-foot stone platform dominated the scene. The platform was lined on three of its sides by overgrown trees and on the fourth by the canyon itself.

"This is absolutely breathtaking," he said.

"And private—that's why it's lasted all these years," she said.

He scanned the view. "That's north, right? Just look at the light on that canyon wall! I wonder how many miles away that is. Mind if I take some pictures? This is great."

"It's three hundred miles. You can take some pictures, but just of the canyon, okay?"

"Sure, I remember—it's a sacred spot." Ramsay pulled his 35mm camera into service and took a few shots. "Man, this is heavenly."

"Marcus, come over here," she said. She knelt and spread out a woven mat in the middle of the stone platform. She took various implements out of her backpack: a feather, a gourd, some wooden kitchen matches, a bundle of herbs, and two leather pouches. She laid them down next to the mat.

"What are those for?" he asked as he removed the camera case from his shoulder.

"You'll see," she said. "I'll walk you through it. For now you need to show me your total trust so I can help you."

"How?"

"Take off your clothes. Except for that ceremonial garment."

"The loincloth?"

"Marcus, you need to trust me. This is only for the

sake of the healing ceremony, I promise you." She patted the mat. "Then, come over and sit here."

Ramsay stood and, feeling self-conscious, took off his T-shirt and shoes, slid off his pants, and left them in a pile. He stood there wearing the leather loincloth and shrugged. "Okay. Total trust, then?"

"Fine. Sit down here." She stood and held her watch up to the rising sun.

"What are you doing?" he asked.

"By pointing the hour hand at the sun, then making an imaginary line between it and one o'clock, I can determine where north and south are." With a pebble, she scratched a three-foot line on the surface of the rock platform.

"Looks like Boy Scout stuff," he said. "How did the ancient Native Americans do it?"

"They used the position of moss next to a tree, the sun, or various stars."

"Smart."

"Wait, Marcus. Watch." She picked up the larger of the leather pouches. She opened it and emptied six colored stones onto the mat.

She picked up one of them. "You must place this stone—the white one—in the north position on the north–south line. North represents strength, spirit, wisdom, and intuition."

He took it from her and put it in its place.

She held up the red stone. "You put this one at the south position, opposite the white one. This represents innocence, trust, and the child within you."

"Where'd you learn all this? Sounds like *Modern Psychology*." He put the red stone in place.

"Native Americans understood sophisticated concepts

that we Caucasians have only learned after hundreds of years of domination. Our concepts are hardly new."

"Incredible."

"A close friend of mine, Daniel Whitehorse—he works here at the park—showed me this ceremony. Since then, I've developed some other ideas. It becomes more powerful when you find what specifics work for you."

"I read once how the Buddha bought into that kind of thinking—the importance of finding your own way."

"There is a universality of thought around the world, you see?"

"From India to the Southwest."

Suzanne spread the remaining stones on the rock surface. "Marcus, you choose your own color for the east. Which would you like?" she asked.

He pointed. "That orange one, I suppose."

She picked it up and put it in the east position. "That one represents illumination, the home of the sacred clown, and the place of the rising sun."

Three stones remained. "Now we only need to use this one." She picked up a black stone and put it in the west position of the yard-wide diamond. "This black one is for the West. It is important in your case. It stands for introspection, sacred dreams, death, and . . . "

"What?"

"Rebirth."

He nodded. "Aha. Makes sense. What about the bowl?"

She poured some ground leaves into the small gourd bowl, lit them, and raised it to the sky. "This is the prayer bowl," she said. "It has an offering of tobacco, a sacred plant. Its smoke carries your prayers to the Great Spirit that dwells in all of us." She reached for the small bundle of herbs and the decorative feather. "Now I light this smudge stick of herbs and blow it out." With the feather, she wafted smoke of the rising smoke at him, then at herself. "I smudge this smoke onto both of us. Now, Marcus, come over into the circle of directions, through the east door."

He stood and walked around her. She put down the smudge stick and led him through the diamond of directions to her side. "Sit here." She took both his hands in hers and looked up at the sky. "Great Spirit," she said. "Please come and bring us to oneness."

"Is this for real, Suzanne?"

"Shh," she said. "Of course. In order to begin the healing process you must clear your mind, open yourself to the availability of the great healing spirit, and have total trust in me. I will be its instrument." She squeezed her eyes tighter.

"Anything wrong?" he asked.

"Wait. I can see the darkness of your pain on my mind-screen. Your ex-wife, your job loss, the rejection you feel in your new life—all of it." She shivered.

"Are you okay, Suzanne?"

"I'm okay . . . but I can see you're not. I can also see that you are not ready to receive the healing. You must be cleansed more deeply. To receive the healing, you must trust the journey I will take you on." She turned to him and, at close range, stared at his skin all over his body, touching him lightly.

He quivered at her touch. "That chills."

"Marcus, you must allow me to touch you freely. My love will be the energy that heals you. You must trust that my love is unqualified. You must feel we are one. Try to relax."

He inhaled deeply, closed his eyes, and sighed. "I just felt a *whoosh*."

"Vulnerability. You are accepting me."

She shook herself out of deep concentration and looked toward the sky. "Look." She pointed up. Azure clouds had accumulated above them.

"That's either coincidence or we have some pretty heavy stuff going on here," he said.

"No joking, Marcus." She spread her arms toward the sky.

"It's raining," he said as cold drops sprinkled on them. Lightning flashed from a mile away. Five seconds later, they heard thunder.

"We only have a few minutes before that storm hits us," she said. "We'll have to wait—"

"Is that hail?" Ice chunks bounced on the rock platform, obscuring Ramsay's view of the canyon.

"Let's leave these things," she said and stood, leaving her pouches, stones, gourd, and herbs on the ground. "Take your camera."

"But leave your stuff?"

"I'll get it tomorrow. For now, let's take cover." She grabbed her pack and ran toward the crevasse in the rock. "Hurry, Marcus."

"Man, that stuff's cold, he said as he put on his pants and shoes. The hail pelted him.

"Get in here!" she said as she waved from the split in the rock.

Ramsay grabbed his T-shirt and camera and ran to the crevasse. He climbed down the little ledge and stood close to Suzanne in the dark. "You're so warm," he said, teeth chattering.

She snuggled up. "You must be freezing." She rubbed the skin on his arms with both of her hands. "Better?"

"Yeah, thanks," he said.

"Let's go," she said. Marcus and Suzanne crawled through the crevasse and waited on the other side for the hail to stop. Once it did, Ramsay followed her up the trail. Just past a turn in the path, Suzanne stopped and looked ahead at the hail strewn on the path. She turned and pushed him hard against the cliff alongside the path. "Wait. I can't."

"Ow. Why'd you do that?" he asked, rubbing his shoulder. "You look terrified."

"Let's stay here for a second." Little bits of gravel fell from the trail, plummeting into the canyon, silently bouncing off sheer cliffs hundreds of feet below.

"You looked totally freaked," he said.

She was breathing heavily. "I'll be okay. Just give me a minute." She held her chest. "This part always gives me the creeps."

"No kidding, it's a long way down there, isn't it?" he said.

She pressed her head into his armpit. "Really."

"You okay now?" he asked.

"Let's get back to my place and get you warmed up."

17

Grand Canyon, Arizona

The steamy shower filled the little bathroom. When Ramsay climbed in, it warmed him instantly. Then the bathroom door opened. It was Suzanne.

"Can I come in?" she asked.

"I guess."

"I mean the shower." She pulled aside the shower curtain and slipped in. "I hope you don't mind. You do need to trust me, you know." She fell into his arms. "Please hold me."

"Uh, sure, Suzanne. Sure." But, reticent, he recoiled.

"I can tell you hate being here with me, don't you?" she asked.

"It's just so sudden. I mean, we're all naked and everything."

"Don't you see, Marcus, you need to trust me and open yourself totally. Only then can I help heal you." She said, "This will help you experience the trust that the ancient Native Americans had. They had no technology, scientific method, nor a need to explain the so-called truth of things. Those are modern conventions."

"I never thought of it that way," he said. "You know, you have real smooth skin."

She smiled and planted a peck on his shoulder. "Trust is everything," she said as she caught the water from the showerhead and dripped it down her fingers, onto his back.

"That feels good."

"Here, let me rub my soap on you." From the tray she picked up two colored discs that smelled like flowers and began to scrub his chest and shoulders, then his sides and belly. She talked as she scrubbed. "The Aborigines have been on the Earth for twenty-five thousand years," she said. "Their culture does not condone or even understand the notion of lying."

"Really?" he asked.

"That's right." She reached behind him and scrubbed his buttocks. "By not accepting anything but truth, they are capable of mental telepathy, even today. They speak only truth—we don't."

"No kidding," he said, and thought about Devlin, Kathy, and his ex-boss.

"We only use truth for convenience, and we excuse our lapses routinely. Then we worship it as if it were some kind of goal we can only aspire to."

"I know what you mean. Say, if I trust you and you trust me—totally—can you tell me what I'm thinking?" he asked.

"That you are capable of understanding truth."

"That's exactly right," he said. "How'd you know?"

She reached up, ran the shower through his hair, pressed her chest to his, and stroked back his wet hair. "Because I am totally open to your spirit, Marcus."

He kissed her, hard but briefly.

"I thought you'd do that," she said.

"Really?"

"Yes. See how that works? Now we're so open with each other that it's acceptable for us to get as close as we can—as soon as we can—without thinking about it," she said. "That's the road to absolute freedom."

"I see," he said. "I think I've felt that before, but only for a moment."

Ramsay felt toasty inside as the water poured over them. He listened to her soft, low voice and watched her eyes—tiny droplets on each lash. He sighed deeply and felt infinitely close to her. "I feel completely at ease with you, Suzanne," he said.

"Come here," she said as she turned off the shower and pulled back the curtain. They dried each other with a fluffy white towel. She took him by the hand and led him to her bedroom.

"Come lie down, Marcus. You feel safe now, don't you?" she asked.

"Yes." He lay on his stomach.

"Good," she said. "Just relax." She sat on top of his buttocks and began to deeply knead his back. After a few minutes of silence, she said, "Marcus, you're so taut. I can feel your pain."

"You can?" he groaned.

"Sure. It's stored in your tissues."

When she hit a particularly tight spot, Ramsay felt vulnerability wash over him as a knot came undone. "Ow!" he cried.

"Go ahead, Marcus. Let it out," she said.

He started to sob. "Why am I crying?"

"You are feeling the pain. It's been there a long time."

"Man-oh-man." He cried more. "I can't believe this."

She massaged him deeply.

"It has become part of who you are—it is your homeostasis, your static state."

He moaned as he explained about his harrowing corporate life in Texas, the contradictions he felt with Kathy, the confusion he had about his attraction to Jessica, and his bittersweet career as a photographer. "Man, I'm so pitiful," he moaned. He slammed the bed futilely.

"What hurts you the most, Marcus?"

"It was so unfair to get fired like that."

"It ripped apart your soul, didn't it?" she said. "The pain is at your very core."

As she pressed hard, he felt weak and experienced a deep sadness. "I cared so much about that company, my career, and helping those people," he said. "It was my reason for living and it was a new beginning for Kathy and me. Why am I crying so hard?"

"You're in touch with your pain. You tried to help them, but were rebuffed. That kind of pain is so deep because your intention was good and the result was so bad. Face your pain, Marcus."

"They just banished me. My boss just spit me out like I was a pumpkin seed—like I was nothing."

Suzanne reached for two tiny bottles. She emptied oil onto the palms of her hands and rubbed it onto him. Then she cuddled him like a mother. "Marcus, don't pumpkin seeds blossom into huge fruit?" she asked.

"I guess," he said. "But I can't see the upside to this pain."

She said, "It's been blocking your happiness for a long time. You need to face it head-on in order to be happy."

Ramsay welled up again. Suzanne gently touched his reddened eyes with circular strokes. Outside, an eagle swooped close to the window and shrieked. "What was that?" he asked.

"An eagle. Just close your eyes," she said.

For a minute, he floated with the eagle, looking at the carved earth of the canyon as it stretched for three hundred miles. He played on currents of air that cradled him as if he were the bird. "I feel like I'm flying through the canyon," he whispered.

"You're okay, she said as she rocked him. "If the bird had been a hawk, it would have been bringing you a message. But it was an eagle—something special."

"How?" he asked.

"An eagle only flies by in the presence of a special one," she said and gently rubbed his eyes again. "You'll understand soon enough."

Then he slept.

18

Grand Canyon, Arizona

When he awoke the next dawn, Suzanne was next to him whispering, "I've been thinking about it all night. I want to be with you now, Marcus."

He looked up. "Be with me?"

"Yes, we are both ready to experience oneness more intimately, being together."

"I admit it was on my mind, but I wasn't sure."

"I am," she said.

It was natural for Marcus Ramsay and Suzanne Dasher to make love slowly and gently. Their eyes locked with each other's. The night of his pool party being close to Jessica had seemed unnatural and forced. Now, the love flowed easily to and from Suzanne. He had known her for only two days, but he found himself almost on the verge of tears as they made love. The more intense their exploration, the more they exposed their emotions to each other.

This is truly a special woman, he thought as they pressed closer to each other.

"You okay?" he asked as they rocked together, never faster than a ticking clock. Her eyes gazed up at him with a relaxed smile of surrender on her lips.

"I love this," she said. "I love you, Marcus—so much."

"Me, too," he said. "I feel so free."

She opened her mouth slightly, closed her eyes, and said, "Ooo."

"Does that please you, my sweet Suzanne?" he asked.

She nodded.

"Your joy is mine." They fell asleep in each other's arms.

Later, a distant church bell rang, waking them. He felt guilty for having loved Suzanne. He explained that he felt he was cheating on Kathy or Jessica or both.

Suzanne toyed with his hair. "Your guilt will pass," she said. "Maybe it's because you were able to surrender your whole self to me."

"That's an understatement, Sweetness."

"You don't love Jesse romantically, do you?"

"No."

"And Kathy?"

"Definitely not—I still long for her. I wish it would've worked, but I know now it never could've."

Suzanne smiled and closed her eyes. "You'll always look back with regret, but you have to move on. Pain from the loss of love lingers."

Ramsay knew his experience with Suzanne had to remain their special secret. Sharing it with Jessica or Kathy would hurt them.

"Can you come to see me next month?" Suzanne asked.

"I don't know, I just don't want Jessica to get hurt."

"I know," she said, "but if our love continues to grow, we'll have to tell her."

He pondered for a second and realized he was no longer afraid of commitment. Having lost Kathy, he had been apprehensive about getting involved in a long-term relationship. He sighed. "Now I feel cleansed and want to make room for you in my life."

She leaned over, kissed him softly on the cheek, and smiled. "I'm so happy."

"You've really helped me get rid of all the garbage."

"Marcus, we didn't get rid of it. It's still there. You've just started to honor your past losses so that you can learn from them."

"Sweetness, I just hope that this doesn't drive a wedge between you and Jessica," he said.

"I love it when you call me 'Sweetness.'"

"You are."

"Marcus, I can tell you are allowing yourself to care about my sister and me. It's proof that the wounds are healing."

As ravens squawked in the dusk, Marcus and Suzanne lounged on the porch after a light dinner.

"Suzanne, being with you has been wonderful. I feel so peaceful. I don't know how to say it—all the bad stuff in my past seems far away."

"I am completed by you, Marcus," she said. "It's been years since I felt this way."

"I just wonder what we can do to keep Jessica from being hurt."

"I'm so glad you're caring for her like that. In the past, you hurt her by judging her. Maybe it was because of your latent anger. Now that's over. You're able to think about her in a new way. You can understand loving unconditionally because your anger is gone."

"I care for Jessica, I guess. I don't really love her, though. But I could grow to like her."

Suzanne hung her head. "Hmm. Marcus, just let your compassion guide you and, don't worry, you will find a way to love her."

"I think I understand." He kissed her. "It's so easy being with you."

"Mmm." They kissed again.

"Suzanne, making love with you was amazing, but just being with you has been unforgettable."

"I know, Marcus. I feel the same." She stroked his cheek.

"It still seems incredible. You've accepted me—failures or not. That's helped me grieve, so I might remember and forget at the same time. Is that how you'd say it?"

"Yes." She smiled. "Honor your losses."

"You've helped me feel how love can be unqualified. I needed to see that was possible."

"Universal compassion." She leaned over and whispered in his ear, "Be led by compassion and your soul will fly endlessly on the wings of others."

As evening turned to darkness, Marcus and Suzanne made love one more time. They flowed together, undulating around each other, kissing and caressing. Afterward, they shared a half-pitcher of sangria and played a simple card game. Marcus looked at his watch.

"Peace be with you," she said as he climbed into his Jeep to leave.

Marcus leaned out the window and kissed her. He sighed. "Sweetness, I can honestly say my life will never be the same."

"Marcus," she whispered in his ear and kissed him passionately. "I love you."

"I love you, too," he said and started the engine.

On the drive home, Ramsay felt a glow. He could picture loving Suzanne for a lifetime. Eventually they would have to tell Jessica about their time together, but he imagined that her reaction would be to start bickering. Maybe she would even refuse to work with him.

As the breeze flew through his Jeep, he thought of Sylvia and how she had been right all along about his need to grieve. He rolled down the window farther.

Suzanne was so attractive in ways that mattered to him. Her graceful movements mesmerized him, and her gentle manner soothed him. Her peaceful soul and deep thoughts helped him look at life in an entirely new way.

She resembled Jessica, but only superficially. Her outdoorsy color glowed, and her bushy, auburn hair made her eyes twinkle. After just a few days, even her hands, ragged and scarred according to Jessica, looked smooth and graceful.

As Marcus drove on, a faint smile formed on his mouth. He reminisced about his teen days when he played music in a band. Now he felt the way a lovely new song must feel: like it was infinite beauty born out of nothingness—now indestructible notes on a page, preserved forever.

19

Marcus Ramsay Photographic, Tustin, California

Ramsay took a break from a shoot later the following week. He walked into his office to finally call Jessica. He had gotten tired of walking around with a pit of paradox in his gut: His relationship with Jessica had only fulfilled him in a quirky, intellectual sort of way, but his once-in-a-lifetime encounter with Suzanne had taken him to an Eden of love and understanding and had helped him cleanse himself of the losses that had taken over his life.

He wasn't sure if it was guilt or compassion that compelled him to reconnect with the first Dasher twin he'd met. He dialed. She picked up the telephone after three rings.

"So, Marcus, what exactly do you want?" she asked in her Chicago twang, a little distant. "Why haven't you called me since your canyon trip? You've been back a week."

"Jessica," he said, "I'm calling now to see how you're doing."

"Well," she said and sighed audibly into the phone, "did you do it with her?"

"Jessica!"

"You did—I know you did."

From his desk Marcus picked up his favorite photo of Suzanne—a five-by-seven taken in the Watchtower—and fiddled with it.

"Jessica, I just wanted to talk. We don't have to have a war."

"Bullshit," she said. "You've never called me just to hear my voice. You hate my voice."

"Did you hear about Devlin?" he asked.

"Changing the subject?"

"No. but, you know, they did find him murdered in his studio: beaten and stabbed—an ugly mess."

"Oh, my God," she gasped.

"I thought you would've heard about it by now. It's been on the news. From the sound of it, he didn't have a second to react."

"Wow," she said. Then there was silence. "Stabbed?"

"Jessica, are you there?" he asked.

Then she talked in a harsh tone: "You are truly an asshole, Marcus! Don't you realize you've single-handedly destroyed our relationship by screwing around with Suzanne?" She hung up.

"What?" *That was sudden.* He set the phone on the cradle. *One twin must have talked to the other.* He decided he'd call Jessica back after giving her a chance to cool down.

The day went slowly. Ramsay felt an uneasy pang grow because Jessica had been so upset.

He felt like calling Suzanne just to hear her voice. He could ask her in a straightforward way if she had told Jessica about them or if, somehow, Jessica had gleaned the truth out of thin air. He also felt like calling Kathy to tell her he had found the perfect woman. Finally he would get the partnership he had been unable to create with her.

Then he pondered how Jessica might've heard the truth from Suzanne—she had probably suffered through every word. No doubt, Jessica had quickly concluded that Ramsay had fallen for Suzanne, when he hadn't even broken a sweat for her.

Jessica must be hurt, he guessed. *No, wait.* Hurt might be an understatement. Having seen how obsessed she was with him, Ramsay figured she must be *decimated* at having lost him to her twin sister.

Ramsay decided to call Jessica back immediately. He would have it out with her, explain everything, and set the stage for a future relationship that could grow in time: sister-in-law—maybe. The phone rang as he picked it up.

"Marcus Ramsay Photographic," he answered.

"Dearie, surprise!"

"Vanessa," he said.

"Listen, honey. Since Stan Devlin died—that must have been an awful mess—ALT Computer would like you to shoot for them next Thursday. Such a huge account—'only the beginning,' they said."

"How'd you find out about Devlin?" Ramsay asked.

"The telly," she said.

"Of course. It's sad that I get the guy's clients after he gets murdered."

"So dreadful. Marcus, you'll need to hire hand talent for this one. It's the main visual in an ad for one of their small medical gizmos. It has something to do with AIDS."

"Jessica Dasher okay for the hand talent?" he asked.

"Whomever you prefer."

"I was about to call her," he said.

"Better call her agent; they want this direct-billed to the client to save the commission."

"Fine."

He hung up and dialed Jessica's agency. A pleasant

voice answered. "Hello, Burret Agency."

"Nancy? Marcus Ramsay here."

"Hi, Marcus," she said. "Hey, bad news about Stan, huh?"

"No kidding. What a way to go. Say, I need to book Jessica for next Thursday—ALT."

"Studio or location?" Nancy asked.

"Studio," he said.

"How many hours?"

"I'm guessing two—make it a half-day. They need this job billed directly to the client."

"Fine. I'll call you back when I confirm her avail'."

Ramsay chatted with Nancy for a while, then hung up.

He went back to the studio and played with a split diffusion shot Tyler had set up. The approach replicated Renoir's style, emphasizing the subject and de-emphasizing the background.

Hours passed.

At about four, when Ramsay had returned from Datachrome with the processed film from his test, he called Nancy Burret again. "Any confirmation on Jessica?" he asked.

"Hi, Marcus. She should have called by now, but she didn't even answer my page—not like her. I'll send someone over to check on her—maybe she's sick. Patti Brackas lives right down the block."

"Who?"

"Patti Brackas. A tall, willowy redhead I use a lot. You should shoot her sometime—a real cutie."

"Fine. Get back to me when you hear something about Jessica," he said. As he hung up, he felt inexplicably nervous because Jessica hadn't called back.

Later, as the sun sank behind the El Toro Tustin Marine Base and the prerecorded tape summoned marines to dinner, the phone rang. Ramsay picked it up.

"Oh, Marcus!" It was Nancy Burret.

"Nancy, what's wrong?" he asked.

"My God . . ." she jabbered into the phone.

"Slow down, Nancy," Ramsay said.

"Patti called me from Jessica's. There were all sorts of voices in the background." Nancy sniffled.

"Voices?" he asked.

"And sirens. She's gone, Marcus. Jessica committed suicide."

"What?" Ramsay asked.

"It's true," Nancy cried into the phone. "She left a note."

"What about?" he asked.

"She felt awful about having done some weird stuff involving her sister and needed to end her pain. I didn't know she had a sister."

"Yeah, a twin," Ramsay said. "Man."

"This is awful, Marcus. What should I do?"

"I have no idea." He shook his head at the phone. "Maybe I should call her family."

"Patti said she OD'd," she said. "Marcus, did you know she was on heavy medication? Antidepressants."

"No. She always acted so hyper."

"That's what I thought."

"Listen, I better go. I need to call her sister," Ramsay said.

"Local?"

"Sort of. Grand Canyon," he said. "Her name's

Suzanne. I just met her when I went over there."

"Oh, I'm sorry, Marcus. This is such a mess. First Stan, now Jessica. I know you liked working with her."

"Her sister's going to die when I tell her the news."

They hung up.

Ramsay sat there stunned. He wasn't sure if he could muster the strength to tell Suzanne. In fact, he couldn't imagine how he'd ever be able to look her in the eye. Everything had changed in an instant.

He pounded the desk. *God, this is too much*, he thought.

Jessica had been so angry at the world, as if she thought it had never approved of her. On reflection, Ramsay felt he could have befriended her more compassionately instead of returning her endless challenges.

Unlike Jessica, Suzanne was at peace, able to see through hypocrisies and even tolerate them. Rather than fight with all that was wrong around her, she flowed with the way things were—good or bad.

Marcus called information, then dialed Grand Canyon's main information number.

"You want Suzanne Dasher?" the woman answered.

"That's right," Ramsay said. "She's a ranger."

"Sorry, all the names are new to me. I just started yesterday. My name is Martha."

"This is very important, Martha," Ramsay said.

"Please hold. It may take a few minutes."

"It's a family emergency."

"Yes, sir," she said. "Thank you."

After a few minutes, Martha came back on the phone. "They're having a problem locating her. I'm putting you through to Daniel Whitehorse, the head ranger."

"Red tape," Ramsay muttered. "Martha, I just saw her two days ago. What could be so difficult?"

"Sorry, Mr. Ramsay. She may be out on a hike. I'll have Daniel talk to you. He's been here for years. He'll know how to find her."

Ramsay twiddled his fingers on the desk and looked at his five-by-seven photograph of Suzanne.

"Mr. Ramsay?" a male voice came on the line.

"Is this Daniel?" Ramsay asked.

"Yes, sir. Daniel Whitehorse. This some kind of joke?" he asked.

"What do you mean?" Ramsay said. "This is a family emergency."

"Emergency? Well, asking for Suzanne's a little inappropriate, don't you think?"

"Why?" Ramsay asked.

"Suzanne Dasher died two and a half years ago in an accident here at the canyon."

"What?" Ramsay asked.

"You must have heard about it—the fall that took her from us."

"But I just—"

"She and her sister were hiking out of the South Rim when she fell."

"I just saw—"

"A real tragedy. They had hiked down a canyon trail and back—hadn't seen each other in years. Suzanne stumbling on that trail was such a freak thing."

"But I just met her."

"That's impossible, Mr. Ramsay. I remember the day like it was yesterday. Afterward, Jessica told me she grabbed Suzanne by the T-shirt but couldn't hold on. She would've fallen, too."

"Incredible," Ramsay said slowly.

"Jesse went into permanent shock afterward. They were real close, you know."

Ramsay began to comprehend how Jessica had pretended to be Suzanne during their magical time together.

Daniel continued, "Jessica always blamed herself for not saving Suzanne. She's always trying to get a job at the park. Doesn't have the right temperment, though. She's not easygoing like Suzanne. Every time she applies, we let her down real easy."

"I remember she told me something like that."

"A year after the accident, I led Jesse through one of my people's healing ceremonies to see if it could rid her of the grief."

"Grief?" Ramsay thought back to his own ceremony. "Daniel, did you know Suzanne well?"

"Oh yes, sir. We talked marriage once, but she wasn't too eager. She said she was looking for some creative type. That wasn't me, for sure." He laughed. "I finally told her I'd let her search for her contentment. She liked the idea, but cried for my loss."

"Cried?"

"Can you imagine? She cried for me after she broke up with me. It was amazing."

Ramsay was silent.

"Marcus? You still with me?" Daniel asked.

"Yeah, I guess. Jessica talked a lot about Suzanne," Ramsay said.

Daniel continued, "Yeah. I can see why. Suzanne and I always remained good friends after we broke up; buddies, you could say. She was the best friend anyone could have."

"I can imagine."

"Say, why'd you say Jesse *talked* about Suzanne?"

"Daniel, Jessica committed suicide today."

"Oh no!" he said.

"She OD'd in her apartment," Ramsay said. "Probably all that Hollywood pressure."

"Bet she never got over losing Suzanne. O Father Spirit, now both Dasher girls are with you. It's a sad day for their folks."

"Yeah," Ramsay said. "Say, thanks for your time, Daniel."

"Wait. How'd you know Jesse?"

"I always shot her hands for ads."

"Ads? You a photographer?"

"Yes."

"Suzanne would've liked you—an artist type?"

"I suppose."

"Do their folks know about Jesse?"

"Not yet. I'll call them," Ramsay said.

"Hyde Park, Illinois, if I remember right."

"Yeah. Suzanne sounds like she was a wonderful once-in-a-lifetime kind of a lady."

"So, she was. Such a shame—both gone."

Marcus thought back to the three days he had spent with Jessica as she convincingly re-created her dead sister.

Daniel said, "Hang in there, Mr. Ramsay. The spirit of someone like Suzanne lives forever—'on the wings' of the rest of us, she used to say. For as long as man's been on this earth, those special people have been here. Eagles appear in their presence, you know."

"I think I've heard that," Ramsay said, thinking back.

20

Marcus Ramsay Photographic. Tustin, California

After an alternative hand model had been auditioned and chosen for the ALT shoot, Tyler and Marcus stood by the "camera table" and tried to sort out the details of the drama that had just unfolded. Still stunned, they took a break from preparing for the shoot.

"Jessica was quite the chameleon," Marcus said. "What you saw one minute wasn't necessarily what you got the next."

"Obviously."

"I always wondered about how she shifted so quickly from one persona to another. Which one was the real Jesse?" Ramsay shook his head.

"None of 'em, I guess," Tyler said. "Or all of 'em. Maybe there was something wrong with her, like multiple personalities."

"Or just severe depression over the loss of a twin."

"Marcus, I can tell you haven't coped with this so good," Tyler said.

"Everything seemed so clear. Now I look back and none of it was real, from the photo clique to Rita to Suzanne. I'm glad I can still count on you."

"Always."

"Thanks, Tyler." Ramsay patted his shoulder.

"You actually never met Suzanne?"

"Nope. She's been gone a couple of years. I guess Jessica was her kachina doll." Ramsay looked up.

"Kachina?"

"It's a long story. I'm just beginning to get it."

Ramsay thought back to the three days he had spent with "Suzanne." *Flying on the wings,* he thought. He closed his eyes.

"What's the matter?" Tyler asked.

"Nothing. Just recalling something a wise woman told me."

Tyler scrunched his nose. "You sure you're okay, Marcus?"

Ramsay felt on the verge of tears. "Yeah. I think I might take some time off to get my head together. Suzanne was just a latent image, I guess. I need to deal with her disappearing from my life like that."

"I'm really sorry, Marcus."

"I think I know what I need to do." Marcus Ramsay slumped out of the studio.

21

Six months later, Marcus Ramsay Photographic

Ramsay's reaction to Jessica's death and the cathartic time he had spent with "Suzanne" made him turn inward over the next few months as he searched for an explanation. Often he would stay at home for several days in a row, thinking about the reality of things.

Every Friday, Tyler took Marcus to lunch at the Barn Restaurant, where, distracted, Ramsay fiddled with his food and mumbled, "Do you realize that everything we experience only exists in our imaginations?" One day Ramsay said, "So, you could say Suzanne was as real to me as if she were alive."

"She really changed the way you see things about life, didn't she?" Tyler asked. "So, she was pretty real."

Ramsay nodded. More introspective now, he had taken on the aura of a devout Asian monk. One week he appeared at the Barn with his hair trimmed to a buzz-cut. He wore an off-white collarless shirt, linen pants, and simple sandals.

After lunch one day, Ramsay returned to the studio and sat at his desk, where he began studying a book on Native American philosophy. The doorbell rang and, moments later, a small group of photographers entered his office and lined up before him.

Ramsay looked up and said peacefully, "Hello."

"Hi." Elise, their spokesperson, stepped forward and said, "Marcus, since you were the first one to put SIP on the map, we think you're the only person who can lead it back to health."

"Please explain that," he answered and folded his hands.

"We think after Stan's death SIP needs a boost and you're it."

Ramsay looked at the group. They were the same people who had ousted him from the board months before. At that meeting they had been reticent to disagree with Stan Devlin.

"Well," Elise said. "We unanimously want you to be our president. What do you think?"

Ramsay spoke softly. "I appreciate your coming to me like this. But I'm afraid I can't help you."

"Why?" she asked.

Ramsay rose. "What you have to offer—the recognition, the service—I no longer need. I'm sorry. You'll have to find someone else. Now, please leave."

They turned and sulked out. Ramsay sat down. He felt a surge of self-worth through his body that lasted all afternoon. He realized that the sadness that had been strapped to him since his corporate debacle had vaporized. A rapture of newness had taken him over.

The euphoria was just dissipating as the sun set. He closed the studio's front door as Tyler's white Blazer squealed to a halt. He got out, carrying a Perry's shopping bag. Ramsay stood there, holding his picture of Suzanne in his right hand and his keys in the left.

"What's so urgent, Tyler?" Ramsay asked.

"Over at Perry's they said it was pretty dramatic the

way you turned down the presidency of SIP—like you were a little crazy."

Ramsay grinned. "We'll see. What are you going to do now, Tyler?"

"Without you? I don't know. Maybe I'll open my own place—go into digital shooting."

"Sounds good. Remember to keep your head up, though. It's easy to see only what you want to see in this business." He glanced down at his five-by-seven picture.

"I've learned so much from you." Tears appeared in Tyler's eyes. "What's that picture?"

"Suzanne, Jessica—whoever." Ramsay smiled and fiddled with it. "Tyler, you'll do great. You have the feel."

"So, what will you do, Marcus?"

"I don't know. I'm floating on an ocean of uncertainty now. I'll hit the land of reality sooner or later."

After they talked awhile, Tyler drove off. Marcus stood outside his locked studio door, rocking back and forth in the dark. He stuffed the crinkled picture into his rear pocket.

Then, tossing his keys from one hand to another, he faced the dark field across Parkway Loop. He squinted into it and fiddled with the studio key until it came off the ring. He wound up like a pitcher and threw it far into the field. He felt all the pressure in him begin to drain away.

He hollered, "Yes!" But there was more to do. He climbed into his Jeep and drove away.

A few minutes later, he was flying east toward Route 40, the breeze in his hair. There was a part of him that needed to soar like an eagle.

22

Grand Canyon, Arizona

Marcus Ramsay drove hard all night toward the canyon. The wind rushed through the open window of the car and dried his tears. He had progressed through the typical stages of grieving for Suzanne: resentment, indignation, bargaining, and anger. He hadn't reached the last step—acceptance of the loss—even if it was only a virtual one.

By the time the sky turned from dense black to steel gray, he had reached the South Rim of the canyon. His eyes puffed from all the weeping.

"Having entered the park, Ramsay rolled down the stony road that led to the Watchtower, where he had taken pictures of her.

He parked near the tower, got out, and walked to the canyon rim. Apparently just out of reach, a palette of muted oranges lit up the distant canyon walls. As he perched on top of a boulder, a chilly breeze whipped at his face. A group of ravens walked behind him, squawking and pecking at the ground for food. He looked over at the tower, recalling the time he had spent with the woman he thought was Suzanne. He closed his eyes and contemplated: "May your soul fly endlessly . . . " she had said to him. Now he knew that to end his emptiness he had to grieve for her in the same way she had taught him to mourn for his other losses.

Excited, he looked across the canyon at the rippled walls as they exploded into bright hues, changing from dark rose to shades of iron and peach, highlighted by tiny blotches of ivory rock, lavender flora, and sea green lichen. The sunrise blossomed as giggles of schoolchildren on an early field trip echoed down the road.

Ramsay climbed off the boulder and walked along the canyon rim until he found the familiar trailhead. He climbed down the steep path and made his way past the point where she had panicked—now he knew why—to the old bush that she had moved aside. He pulled it back and squinted into the dark, then shimmied sideways through the split in the rock. Morning light appeared at the end of the tunnel. He climbed onto the sandstone platform that overlooked the canyon. He remembered how trees and bushes lined three sides and the canyon bordered the fourth—it was the Hopi special place.

He walked to the spot where she had led him through the healing ceremony. At his feet lay the four Hopi ceremonial stones for north, south, east, and west. The prayer gourd and the smudge stick of herbs lay there amid the stones. Suzanne had left them behind when his ceremony was interrupted by hail. She had never come back to retrieve them.

Now Ramsay felt an urgent need to re-create the ceremony. He stripped to his underwear, knelt, lit the smudge stick, and blew it out. He wafted some of the smoking herbs into his face. He looked down at the herbs, held together by several strands of old leather cord. As he began to feel lightheaded, he heard a screech and looked up, but there was no eagle.

"Damn," he called. "Where are you?" He cried out, "Oh, where are you, Sweetness?" He remembered how the eagle had appeared in Suzanne's presence, signaling his need to recognize and honor his old wounds. Now, he was grieving over his loss of her, and he needed to own that. His heart ached—it always would.

"To the north, to the south . . . ," he called to the sky as she had. "To Father Spirit." He opened his eyes. "Nothing! I can't do this!" he shouted. Then he pulled one of the leather thongs until it broke. The charred herbs sprayed through the air.

"Shit." Before he stood, he reached over and pulled the crumpled five-by-seven photo of Suzanne from the back pocket of his discarded jeans. Her image smiled at him with ivory teeth. The whites of her eyes glowed.

That's it, he thought. When his original grieving ceremony had been interrupted by hail, she had explained that wounds were only meant to be stored, never forgotten. He had to honor his grief and claim it first. He would never forget it.

He reached down and picked up the small black stone that had symbolized rebirth during his ceremony. He knew what he had to do now. He shook, excited.

He wrapped the rock with the photo, like a little Christmas present. He had just found a way to honor his grief, yet put it away temporarily.

He held the little package with both hands, closed his eyes, and shouted into the breeze, "Sweetness, your memory will always dance in my heart!" A chill rushed through him as he saw an eagle appear in his mind's eye.

"Suzanne, it's you." He sighed deeply and hung his head as he fondled the little bundle. "For now, I have to say good-bye to you," he said, "and tuck you away so I can go on. But every time I search my heart, I will remember the loss of you, for there is no getting over grief—only putting it aside."

Ramsay looked out at the canyon and cocked his right arm. As he heaved the little package into the breeze, he wailed a long, guttural yell: "Sweetness!"

Time stopped. He thought of Kathy, his old job, and his banishment from the photo community. He was finally leaving the hurt from all of them behind. He thought of Jessica—not the Jessica who played her sister, the real Jessica. He felt a pang in his heart as he recalled her quirky ways. At that moment he realized that the grief from the losses would always be near him: in a safe place, along with the pleasant memories.

The rock sailed up into the air with the leather thong whirling behind it, then out into the canyon. Carrying the crumpled five-by-seven photo as its wrapping, the rock curved gently downward, increased speed, and flew from Ramsay's sight.